PLUTO,
animal lover

PLUTO,
animal lover

a n o v e l

LAREN STOVER

■ HarperCollins*Publishers*

HarperCollins books may be purchased for educational, business, or sales promotional use. For information, please write: Special Markets Department, HarperCollins Publishers, Inc., 10 East 53rd Street, New York, NY 10022.

FIRST EDITION

Designed by C. Linda Dingler

Library of Congress Cataloging-in-Publication Data
Stover, Laren.
    Pluto, animal lover : a novel / Laren Stover. — 1st ed.
      p.   cm.
    ISBN 0-06-017111-1
    1. Young men—New York (N.Y.)—Fiction. 2. Mentally ill—New York (N.Y.)—Fiction. 3. Animal welfare—New York (N.Y.)—Fiction. I. Title.
PS3569.T6736P55 1994
813'.54—dc20   93-42869

94 95 96 97 98 ❖/RRD 10 9 8 7 6 5 4 3 2 1

For Paul Gregory Himmelein,
Gertrude, my grandmother, &
Cap, who's pushing clouds.

I'd like to thank Molly Friedrich, who moves like lightning; Renata Miller and the Writers Room for sanctuary; the Ludwig Vogelstein Foundation; Barry Sherman, my first and favorite voice of Pluto; my copper-haired conductor, Susan Shacter; Elyse Connolly for putting bird in hand; Craig Carlisle and the Naked Angels Theater; the Cornelia Street Cafe; Giles Blunt, relentless structural adviser; Julie Moline, feverish typo teacup; my editors, Craig Nelson, the unflappable Aquarius who started the fire, and Robert Jones, the Pisces who kept the coals burning and walked barefoot over them; and Geneviève Geer, goddess of my animal psyche.

PLUTO,
animal lover

My name is Pluto. My mom had this idea that all her kids would have names of planets and elements, stuff like that. She had six classic hippie names picked out for the six kids she planned to have. Rain, Trout, Luna, Tree and Galaxy. She and my dad, Hercules Gerome, tried to have more children. Hercules wanted eight, or was it ten? But Mom had a miscarriage after me, and some other female complication, so I ended up being the only one she got to name. After a while, she said she wished she'd named me Trout or Tree instead. She said after she'd read more about Pluto, she thought it was a negative name, destined to be unhappy in love.

Hercules left before I was two and went off with a girl named Bubbles from Baltimore. Mom would never talk about Bubbles. Secretly, I liked her name. It had an effervescent and transient quality, maybe shallow, but probably guaranteed a good time.

I have to admit, Mom's thing for names rubbed off on me. I make it a habit not to know people with plain names, especially nicknames. That's the reason I don't have many friends. Too many common Joes. And forget girls. Whenever I meet a girl it's always Mary, Debbie or Sue. But I'm not unhappy, I get along fine. I had a double major in English and biology at Tulane, moved to New York, and got a job at a medical publishing house—Eagle Press—where I copyedit a pancreas journal. I'm one of the only men there. My boss, the managing editor, Camillia, says I have "unusual sensitivity for a straight man." I wonder why she thinks I'm straight. I never talk about girls. Maybe she's seen some of the magazines I buy. I don't make any effort to hide them. *Legs. Puritan.* But no, that must not be it. Why would a sensitive man want to ogle beaver? I buy them hoping I'll find something arousing, but I never do. Well, rarely. There was a great photo once of a woman in strappy heels stepping on a garter snake.

I live alone, but I'm not lonely. I've got pets. Stripemaster and Stalin, the garter snakes, Kilroy, the chameleon, my omnivorous fish, an oscar named Bacteria, a tank full of little fish for Bacteria's meals, I gave up naming them all, I just couldn't keep up with the turnover, and Sunshine, a good-natured raven—Mom asked me to take care of her for a while—I wish I could keep in a diaper. My pets depend on me. What bothers me sometimes is people.

~

This is the first thing I remember. When I was about two my stepfather crouched down on the bathroom floor, the light was all yellow, and held my little painted turtle upside down. The eyes were like shiny buttons, blinking, and the legs were like little hands with nails, webbed hands, I remember thinking that, and my stepfather opened its little pointy mouth with a can opener and poked around until something popped. He dropped the turtle in the toilet and I put my hand in to get him back but then he flushed it, and I watched its shell swirl down, pretty as spin art, which I make, by the way. I rigged up my turntable and spin art on 78.

My stepfather's name is Bill. If Mom had had kids with Bill, they'd be named Bob, Dan and Dick.

One good thing about Bill. Sometimes he had a sense of humor. Like the time Judy Baker, the neighborhood redhead came over with Raggedy Ann, a dumb-expressioned doll unfortunate enough to wear its heart on its chest, I gave it a nap in a sleeping compartment in the lower berth of the oven. Bill set it at 350 degrees.

~

My office is near an animal shelter. At lunch I volunteer to walk dogs. One day I ran into Camillia while I was walking Noel, the sheepdog.

"Aren't we secretive, Pluto. I didn't know you had a dog. All those talks we have about our pets."

"We don't," I tell her. "I use my lunch hour to walk homeless animals from the shelter over there," I say dutifully, turning so she can see the back of my jacket, the one the shelter gives walkers to wear. It says, "ASPCA DOG WALKER."

This may be one reason she thinks I'm sensitive. I don't tell her about my pets. That's personal. I've listened to her talk about hers, though. Some people think listening means you've had a two-way conversation. Taureans are like that.

She's not sensitive the way a Virgo is. I'm a Virgo. The sign ideally suited for paying attention to minute details. For listening. For helping animals and people in distress. Virgos make good doctors and nurses, they say, though this was never my idea of a good job—too much human contact. I thought about becoming a vet. But my ambition in life, my main ambition, is to help out animals in an artistic way. Even animal artifacts should be dealt with creatively. I have a skull and bone collection, and when tissue is left on bones, a steer skull or a sheep skull, roadkill or whatever, it not only looks messy but that decay odor is vomitile. So I import these beetles from a catalogue to eat off the remaining flesh. I could use acid, but using beetles seems sensitive to ecology. That's what I mean about a Virgo being sensitive. We think of things like that. And we're very clean. That's another attribute of Virgos. What makes me a little different from most Virgos is my moon. It's in Scorpio. A lot of books say that's bad. Sadistic. But I figure it makes me a little more uncommon. Like a special birthmark or a missing limb.

I don't think a plain Virgo would put beetles to work on skulls in a bathtub, but actually, it's a practical idea if you don't have a place outside to do it. It's not like I don't clean the tub out with bleach afterwards. That's why it's great having my own bathroom now. I can put stuff in the tub without Mom having a fit. And everything's clean and organized, with no toothpaste splatters on the mirror. No more feminine hygiene products. No more stench of the new father, Bill's black hairs left curling on the Camay. When he arrived from Manshack, a small town a few hours away over a long spit of phlegm-colored water, there was a new smell. A phony cleanliness covering something dark and fungal. This morning I woke up and showered using frankincense-and-myrrh soap. It was expensive, but I'm not an Irish Spring kind of guy. I shave in the shower so the steam can soften my beard. It's not much of a beard, pale blond and thin. The bleached-out Scandinavian features of my mother won out over the Greek and French genes of my father, except for my eyes. They're a seventies color, not really brown. Maroon.

One of the goldfish was floating in the bowl when I got up. Bacteria will never eat a dead fish. Oscars have enough sense to know a dead fish could be diseased. And where's the fun?

That reminds me of something else that happened when I was a kid. Mom and Bill have gone out and I'm in the house alone. I push a chair over to the aquarium in the kitchen. Then I get on the chair and watch the fish swimming in circles in their small bubbling tank, horrible endless circles of perpetual meaninglessness, the monotony broken only by sucking in the food Mom sprinkles in. I reach in and catch the black fish with the bulging eyes, and then the gold ones, and put them on the floor and watch them until the fins stop fluttering. Peace at last. I think this was the blossoming of my altruistic instincts.

Mom is mad when she gets home, then cries. She used to cry a lot back then. She gets a Sucrets box and we put the fish, Heaven, Moon and Bambi, on a piece of Kleenex and bury the box in the field behind the project where we live right across from the Saint Louis II cemetery on the outskirts of the French Quarter. Bill doesn't come with us. Mom takes a flashlight and we walk outside and I like the dark humid sounds my shoes make on the grass.

The Sucrets box will pop up, most likely, because of the Louisiana water table, after the heavy rains. The Devereauxs buried their grandmother in the miasmic soil in their yard just like she'd wanted, in her wedding dress, and the body surfaced that spring, her bloated and decayed flesh glistening under the shade of the palmettos with a supernatural beauty. Too bad. It was such an efficient way to dispose of a body, and embalming always seemed a bit gruesome to me, not to mention unnatural.

I went to the shelter today. I feel bad for every animal in there. Every one of them has been abandoned. I'm thinking about getting another pet. It won't be any trouble to get approval. They all love me over there. I looked at the dogs. The cats. And the room with all the weird animals.

It's always hard to find weird animals homes. Like the weasel. Who wants a two-year-old weasel that sometimes bites? Or a rabbit with one ear? A skink with three legs? Or the boa constrictor that ate a litter of kittens?

Maybe I'll start with the weasel.

~

When I got to work this morning I heard Camillia scream.

"It's still alive, oh my god, it's still alive." So I go into her office and apparently the exterminators who were there last week put down sticky traps and a field mouse is stuck in one, practically ripping its foot off to free itself.

I get a legal pad and rip the cardboard off the back and shove it under the trap.

"What are you going to do with him?" Camillia wails. She's got on a new outfit that I can tell she thinks is sexy in a power trip kind of way. A short red skirt. The red power suit. I hate red.

"Where are those gloves the trash guy uses?" I ask her. Camillia tells me to look in the janitor's closet and I find the gloves, put them on and take the mouse into the men's room.

The first thing I do is put soap in the trap. Then water. The mouse is wriggling and squeaking. It's amazing how loud something so little can be.

The door opens as I'm working to get my tie clip under the mouse's foot.

"What the fuck, what are you, fucking crazy?" Joey, the mailroom boy, comes in. "Kill the fucker."

He grabs my shoulder to get a better look and the tie clip, a silver grinning monkey in a top hat, jabs into the little foot. The water makes the blood run until the liquid in the trap is pale red.

"Hey, moron," I tell him, "Now look what you made me do. This little guy has as much right to live as you do."

"It's a fuckin' mouse, man, a disease-carrying rodent."

"You know," I tell him, "you're brainwashed. You buy that crap that humans are so much better than animals, especially animals you can have some sort of power over."

But I feel like a wire is coiled in my stomach, like it's winding and building up pressure and getting so tight it will spring out in a minute and kill everybody in the way.

I'm still holding the mouse and I look at Joey's face. There's a cruel curl in his upper lip that reminds me of

Elvis Presley gone wrong. He's wearing a tight bicycle racing jersey so you can see all his muscles, jeans a little too small and running shoes.

I wear Hush Puppies. Tan. I believe in handsome but comfortable shoes. That's one of the benefits of having been raised in the South. It makes you civilized. Half the guys in New York wear casual shoes. Worse than casual. I find sport shoes loathsome unless the sport is being performed. If I were a girl I'd never date a guy in basketball or running shoes. Unless he was Michael Jordan. Or Shaquille O'Neal.

"What are you looking at me like that for?" Joey says. He takes a couple of steps back. His shoes squeak. The mouse's leg is severed and probably the humane thing to do is put it out of its misery.

"You're right, Joey." I put the trapped mouse on the floor. The trap is filled with soapy blood. I imagine the coil gorging through his jersey and his intestines unraveling like wet shiny Christmas ribbon.

"I'm wearing my good shoes," I tell him. "Do me a favor and kill the fucker." You have to speak their language, you see.

Joey doesn't do anything for a minute. The mouse screams. Joey looks at the trap. He puts a couple of paper towels over it. The mouse is moving so frantically it pushes them off. He puts down some more. The mouse is quiet now. Then Joey stares at me and slams his foot down on the mouse, staring at me the whole time like he's getting off on killing while I'm watching. There's a faint wheezing sound. He slams his foot down again. My palms are sweating. The coil in me releases and I feel incredible, like I just had an injection of speed.

I always thought needles were pretty cool, gleaming, silvery, sharp. A swift way to give a vaccine or antidote. Or put something to sleep.

~

Wanda. Today I brought the sheepdog in as Wanda was taking the two Pekingese. She'd brought them rhinestone collars. Girls love to put things in collars and hold on to them.

Wanda is sparrow-thin with long bony poetic fingers and no polish. The receptionist at the ASPCA told me Wanda has quite a collection of pets. She has two cats, a rabbit, two marmosets, a lemur, I bet that's illegal, and red hair. I think about petting her hair, running my hand along the waves. I bet she's a Pisces.

She doesn't screw around with her hair as far I can

tell. Some guys don't seem bothered by girls bleaching, streaking, crimping and perming their hair. But it really bugs me. My mother never did anything to her hair. She wore it blonde and straight. Chuck in the circulation department chooses girls strictly by hair color. Chuck's balding and bowlegged and walks with his hands in his pockets, which rips the pockets, my mom always said. He's in his forties and still chews gum, not even sugarless. "She's a blonde," he'll say, as though that sums up a girl's qualities. All he ever talks about is girls. Blondes, of course, and tits. He takes magazines into the men's room. Never anything cool, though, like the *Police Gazette* or the *Weekly World News*.

I'm always cordial, naturally, but Chuck feels like he has to make comments like, "Hey stud? How come I never see you with any babes?"

It's not so easy to find a girl who lives up to Mom.

God, I miss her.

Poor thing. On antidepressants even before I was born. Everything she loved left or died. Like Moonbeam, the miniature poodle. Mom had him freeze-dried, the eyes were glass, of course, and sealed in a case on the coffee table. It died of natural causes. Mainly Bill.

~

I like girls natural. Wanda Swann. She has a great name. I've seen it in the ASPCA sign-up book. I'm going to ask her over to dinner when I see her again. Maybe I should get another set of eating utensils and another plate. Maybe I should have her stop by the office so people don't think I'm queer. No. Not a good idea. What if the relationship doesn't work out?

~

I just had this dream. I'm in the subway and instead of tracks it's concrete ravines with some water. Dead puppies and kittens, their stomachs bloated, are floating in the water, washed up on the edges. The fire department's there but they're not doing anything. I see a small Lab, a pale one, still alive. On the other side of the ravine, Wanda's dangling a rhinestone collar. She's wearing a long white dress with red blotches. "You're out of control," she says, waving the collar.

This is another memory. I'm about eight. I pick up the corpulent cat Lullabell by the neck and listen to her gag. I get a weird feeling in my stomach. Lower than my stomach. Like that coil-about-to-spring feeling. She struggles but doesn't scratch me. I loved that cat. She slept with me. I had to keep myself from squishing her too hard, I loved her so much. The neighbors on St. Ann Street had a cat, Big Tom. He was a manx. He was mean to Lullabell. He tormented her. One night they got into a fight and Big Tom scratched her eye and bit into her leg. She limped home. Big Tom's family said if we were so concerned about our precious cat we should keep her inside. The bite got infected and Lullabell stopped eating. Bill said when an animal stops eating it wants to die. Mom said, "Please, Bill, she needs to go to the vet."

Bill said, "Sixty-five bucks or whatever on a cat that'll most likely die?" I tried crying into the cut, which was turning blue with parts that looked like a turnip, because I'd heard that tears could heal a wound.

Lullabell crawled in my bed and put her head on my pillow just like a little person, and died. I didn't tell Mom and Bill. After half a day she got stiff but she still had her fur smell and I loved her despite the fact that she was completely unresponsive. I thought when she started to go really bad I could have her stuffed. I thought maybe I could do it.

I didn't get the idea of what to do to Big Tom until after Mom found Lullabell, cried, then asked Bill to take care of it. "We can't afford to have her freeze-dried, honey," Mom said. That's when it hit me that there would be no justice, unless I did something myself.

I think Wanda might understand this feeling of revenge. She seems sympathetic. But I'm digressing.

I waited for the family on St. Ann to be away. I got some string, work gloves and some of Bill's tools. I took a piece of liver and let Big Tom smell it. I tried to get him to follow me but he kept stopping and just sitting. I went back home and got Lullabell's carrying case from the closet. I went out and found Big Tom again and let him see me put the liver in it. The cat circled the cage and finally stuck his anvil-shaped head in. Then I pushed him, because I didn't feel like waiting anymore. He started yowling, but then stopped. I could see he was eating the liver, the little pig. I walked with him around the cemetery and past a field and an empty warehouse. I kept walking until we were in another neighborhood. I went over a low metal fence past a playground and into some woods. I opened the cage very slowly but Big Tom tried to run out, so I subdued him with the hammer. His eyes rolled back in his head. I wasn't sure if I'd do what I planned but then

I thought of Lullabell on my pillow and how lonely I felt. I held him real tight and looked for a wide tree. I put on the gloves. Then I pushed Big Tom against the tree and tied twine around him. His breath smelled like liver. Bad breath has always bugged me. He started to wriggle but I made it real tight. He tried to scratch me so I kicked him pretty hard. Then I sat back for a minute and watched him squirm on the tree and I was proud I could tie something up and it would stay, like in a movie. I felt like a cowboy.

I took out some nails and stretched out the cat's right arm. I pushed a nail into the tough little black pad and the cat screamed. I pounded it in with the hammer and blood gushed out in a perfect arc. I felt strong. Dramatic. I remember thinking, "Hey, this is it." I tingled all over. How would I explain that sensation to Wanda?

I don't see Wanda for two weeks because she's on vacation. She told the receptionist at the shelter.

"Where did she go?" I ask him.

"Las Vegas," he says, "with a guy. Wish it was you?" And he winks. Not to the Elvis Chapel, I hope. I hate that when people get familiar with me but I just smile. If you're polite, no one knows what you're thinking.

It's hard to be polite sometimes. Like with Camillia today.

"After you edit this, make sure these pictures are right side up," she says. "And key the headings, would you?" She slaps some layouts on my desk, which is immaculate, by the way, no pencil marks, and everything in its place. She gives me an article on mumps infecting human fetal pancreatic islet-like cell clusters when she knows I wanted to work on the diabetic rat findings. Animals have always fascinated me. I used to have these great fantasies about wrapping ibis and cat mummies. Extracting their vital organs and pulling the brains out through a nasal cavity without making a single scratch on their skulls. Embalming them with fragrant resins and oils. I bet those dead animals smelled like a million bucks.

Wanda smells clean. She doesn't try to impress people with status perfume. I bet her desk, if she has a desk, is clean, too. I know we were destined to meet. She has red hair. I have red eyes. Red. Like a valentine. Like a rabbit heart still beating in the vetivert-scented weeds after a cat's ripped it in two. I wonder if Wanda sings. Not to Madonna stuff with a Walkman on. She's not the type to have one of those. But real singing. Pretty songs. Old stuff. Maybe like the songs my mom sang.

A week goes by. I see Wanda as she's leaving the shelter.

"Going so soon?" I ask.

She smiles. "I don't believe we've officially met."

"My name's Pluto Hellbender Gerome," I say and extend my hand. She's bound to notice how clean my nails are. That I have a writer's bump, a sign of intelligence.

"Pluto. Wasn't he the god of the underworld? I've seen you around. I'm Wanda Swann."

Her hands are smooth and cool and her handshake's firm. Not the dead fish handshake of some girls.

"I've seen your name in the register," I say. "I thought it was beautiful. Now I know who it belongs to."

She thinks I'm handsome. I can tell. But she seems a little nervous. I must be coming on too strong. I've got to be cooler. Damn. I keep forgetting, women never go for nice guys, guys who buy roses and always call when they say they will. Women are more excited by liars, cheats and serial killers.

"Well, see you around," I say and turn to go into the shelter.

She leans toward me. I can smell the cleanliness. Ivory soap. And something faintly floral.

"Do you work near here?"

"Yes," I say. "About nine blocks away." I nod toward the west so she can get a good look at my angular chin. "And you?"

"Not far from here either." She nods. She has a chin like mine, like Mom's. "I have a part-time job at a music store. But it's just a job. One of my jobs."

"What else do you do? Anything interesting?"

"No. No, not at all." She seems really nervous now, like this is a touchy topic.

"I'm really a composer. It's just hard, you know, to make ends meet so I have these jobs. Just until something works out. I'm applying for a New York Foundation of the Arts grant. "

"Good luck," I tell her. I smile sincerely. "What else do you do then, waitress?"

"No, not that, I don't waitress. I never actually wait on people."

"I know what you mean. People aren't worth it."

"Well," she says and looks behind her like she's afraid somebody will hear her, "I sort of entertain."

"Do you sing?" I ask. "Is your music sad? God, I hope it's sad. My mom," I tell her, "used to rock me to sleep singing Irish and English folk songs. Billy was hanged by a long golden cord though his lover lamented he was innocent. I pictured Billy dangling from a shimmering chain like a paper Christmas ornament beneath the trembling leaves of the tallest tree in the cemetery.

Spanish moss brushed his forehead, his hair, pale like my mother's, like mine, while graceful vultures cast shadows with their majestic wingspans. Love has always been the Siamese twin of tragedy."

I figure a girl will be moved by this sensitive but cryptic display of poetic thought. She must have been really moved because she kind of backs off, smiling faintly like she's too choked up to talk.

I have romantic thoughts about Wanda tonight. Wanda coming over to my bachelor pad and admiring Bacteria. Wanda commenting on how clean my apartment is. It's the kind of place a girl could love. No James Dean posters for me. My bedroom walls are almost completely papered with photos of animals—kittens, ducks, cute things and a few endangered species. I imagine Wanda loving my spin art, noting the deliberately vibrant color clashes. Wanda cooing she's never seen a more stunning skull collection. Wanda beside herself when she realizes she's met a guy who uses frankincense-and-myrrh soap.

I have to think of a romantic place to take her for our first date. Like maybe the zoo.

On Saturday I check out the petting zoo at Coney Island. I thought we could get really close to the animals there. God, it was awful. Hoards of kids are at the chick incubator tapping on the glass. Poor little peeps. All those drooling, vulgar children squishing their runny noses against the glass and banging on it, day in and day out, seven days a week, imprinting the baby chicks with their grape-juice-stained aggression. This is no way to live. Somebody, I'm thinking, ought to quietly pull out the plug to the heater. Sure, they'd huddle pathetically and shiver and die. But it wouldn't be long before they'd be out of their misery.

I felt most wound up when I saw the rabbits, sheep, goats and llama. Children are actually allowed to physically molest them. Encouraged, even. What kind of a person thought up this petting zoo concept? Some kind of a sadist. I feel altruism building up a beautiful tension in my lower body. This just might be my mission in life.

I'm not exactly sure what I'll do yet. In the meantime I take the weasel that sometimes bites home from the animal shelter. I make a list of possible names:

Medusa.
Rasputina.
Eva Braun.
Jaws.

I decide on Le Sang. She'll be needing her distemper shot in about two weeks, they said. Perfect. I have things to do at the vet's.

~

When I get in to see the "exotic" specialist at the Animal Medical Center, I take Le Sang out of Sunshine's birdcage. An intern, you can tell it's an intern by the eager expression, comes in to weigh her and declares, "Well, isn't Let's Sing precious."

"Le Sang," I tell the intern. "Her name's Le Sang." I guess it's too much to expect a New Yorker to know any French. If I punctured her arm right now she'd learn. That would be a perfect way to teach her. I'd tell her, smiling, "*Sang* is French for blood, got that?"

The intern smiles broadly and weighs the weasel. She bends over to listen to her heart and Le Sang bites the stethoscope.

"It's the rubber," I shrug. "She goes wild over rubber."

The intern leaves me pinning down the weasel, who is squirming to get out of my hands on the stainless-steel table, where I can see the open stainless-steel sliding cabinets gleaming. I see syringes and drugs. Le Sang struggles, her nose twitches. I figure she'll calm down a little if

I let her smell something new. Like the cabinet. There must be some rubber in there. My heart starts to beat too fast, totally adrenalized, just thinking about what I'm going to do. I hold her in one hand and she lurches forward as I go over and grab a handful of syringes. I drop them casually into my leather briefcase as though I'm meant to have them, as though they're rightfully mine because the virtue of my future actions will far outweigh this small transgression. I have a sense of purpose now.

I also see two neuroleptics I recognize, major tranquilizers, Tanax and Fatal Plus, the best thing to put animals to sleep. I take just about all of it. Who's to know?

The vet comes in as I'm closing my case. I smile easily. She smiles back and strokes Le Sang between the ears. She listens to Le Sang's heart as I hold her mouth shut, and then feels her belly. She inspects her ears and comments she's never seen a ferret with shinier fur. What do I feed her, she asks. "Iams Cat Food," I tell her, "and sometimes I make a special meal with egg yolk."

I don't tell the vet what the other ingredients are. That I try to re-create what the weasel might eat in the wild. Pulverized bugs and white mice. Cooked, of course. We can be imaginative cooks, health, of course, being the priority. People often underestimate the creativity of Virgos.

Le Sang is uncomfortable with all this probing. I hold her under the feet and by the scruff of the neck so she'll be more docile. The vet gives her the injection and as she withdraws her hand, Le Sang whips her head around and bites the vet through the rubber glove.

"Rubber," I smile.

The vet smiles insincerely and says that will be all for today and then takes off the gloves and washes her punctures. Being a vet is not such a great job. You can't discipline the animals.

Since the petting zoo is out of the question, datewise, I've thought of another place to take Wanda. Pet World is doing psychic readings for animals on Halloween. I tell Wanda when I see her at the ASPCA. She sounds enthralled, says she never heard of anything like it.

"It's downtown. I'll pick you up," I tell her.

"That's okay," she says, not wanting me to go out of my way. "I'll meet you there if I can make it."

"Two o'clock," I say.

She smiles. Her teeth look like a toothpaste ad. Straight, white, and never any particles of food stuck in them. I bet she brushes her teeth after lunch like I do. Her lips have the same sort of swell as the young Marlon Brando, the kind of mouth, if her breath isn't bad, I could almost imagine kissing.

I put Le Sang in Sunshine's birdcage and get there exactly at two o'clock. Virgos like to be on time. I can't believe I haven't asked Wanda what sign she is.

The psychic has a little table set up with a black cloth over it. The cloth is embroidered around the edges with whales, dolphins, fish, planets and stars.

She doesn't look psychic. And I don't place much value on something so unscientific. A psychic reading can't possibly be as accurate as an astrological reading. Astrology is a science. Desperate people seek psychics. But hey, it's a date. Wanda and I are supposed to have a good time. I guess this is one of those reckless things that people are supposed to do when they start to fall in love.

Where is Wanda, anyway? She must be a Pisces. They're always late.

A woman with honey-colored dreadlocks and a black kitten gets up from the table. The woman's arms are covered with silver bracelets and scratches. The kitten hisses and takes a swipe at her eye. "Chill, Cleopatra," says the woman. "Chill or I kill."

Some people aren't fit to have pets.

By the time I've read the ingredients on every package of pet food in the store, including all the pet vitamins, it's nearly twenty past two and Wanda's still not here. Why did she smile at me like that if she wasn't coming? Did she forget? Did one of her pets take ill?

I pull the chair out quietly and sit down, making eye contact with the so-called psychic.

"I feel," she says, "I feel pain connected to this animal. Causing pain." She yanks her hand away from Le Sang.

"She bites, doesn't she?" she says, looking at me.

Le Sang just sits there, calm for a change. I don't say anything. Why should I give her any clues?

"I have a sense of her being in a tiny cage. Locked up. Someone, several people owned her before you.

"I see more pain," she says. "Pain to the animal."

She seems to forget that Le Sang bites and she picks up her front paw.

"Here," she says, pointing to the webs between her claws. "I see pain here. And something else very disturbing. It's just not coming up."

"You like to be with animals, don't you," she says to me. "I see you surrounded with animals. You think they will make you happy, give you some sort of pleasure. They do. But there's something, something sad about this. There's something else I see in the near future. I'm seeing a dog you'll encounter in another city. In the South. I know this sounds too strange to be true, but the dog is pink."

Wanda never shows up. Maybe she got the date wrong. That could mean she's an air sign. Bad news for a Virgo. It's hard enough just trying to keep myself organized. It would have been romantic, our knees touching under the black cloth. She would have brought her neurotic Abyssinian, and the psychic, seeing us in the throes of love, would have given Wanda a reading to complement mine, like maybe she'd predict Wanda would see a green bear. This wouldn't mean anything obvious like I'm going to shoot some ducks at a carnival and win her animals. It's a metaphor for the sense of fantasy we evoke in each other. The psychic's bound to notice how in tune we are with each other, and when people pick up on love, it's infectious. It brings out the largesse in a person. Seeing us in love would compel her to give us colorful animals, a sign of hope.

I'd offer to walk Wanda home and she'd be a little hesitant but demurely say "yes," and then she'd invite me up to see her pets—her doorman would bow when I walked in—and I'd see how tasteful her apartment is, and how clean. A relationship is possible if you don't find socks on the floor and dishes in the sink and the soap in the bathroom's not sitting in a puddle of water in a soap dish.

She'd offer me tea, something English or healthy like camomile. It wouldn't be coffee, I'm sure she doesn't drink coffee, but I'd say, "Another time," and when her neurotic Abyssinian and pristine Persian brushed affectionately against my leg I wouldn't even worry about the cat hair on my trousers until I got home, where I have two lint removers, one in the closet and one in the kitchen.

Later that evening the phone rings. Who the hell is calling me? Wanda maybe, to invite me over for tea? Or Camillia to tell me I've done a great job, that my silent, methodical, precise work has not gone unnoticed? Or maybe it's the vet's, there could have been a video camera in the room, I looked but I must have missed it, and when they did inventory and found stuff missing they reviewed all the tapes and tracked me down. The possibilities are unlimited—it could even be a wrong number. I hate these unpredictable situations, things out of your control, but I decide to answer, to do it with control in my voice. I even make my voice kind of upbeat, like I'm having a nice and guilt-free day, and I pick up the phone like I've got nothing to hide and say,

"Pluto Hellbender Gerome here, how may I help you?" And it's Mom. She's in the hospital again and wants me to visit.

"You can stay with Bill," she tells me, but I say, "No thanks, I already have a place in mind. A revamped mansion in the Garden District, $35.00 a night."

"Well, at least you won't be anywhere near that dreadful Bourbon Street," Mom says. She ought to know how dreadful. The poor thing had to get a job at one of the clubs when Bill was out of work for a spell. Like six years. She wore hiphugger bell-bottoms in transparent red, white and blue. I sat alone, usually, spinning on a barstool and staring up at the ceiling fan and drinking root beers and ale and eating peanuts, which of course I now know can cause colon cancer. The ceiling fan had three different speeds and I was glad, sort of, when it got faster, at least at first, because then I could get dizzy and not think about Mom. Not that Mom didn't look beautiful. I just couldn't stand the way men stared at her.

I tell Camillia I'll take some pancreas work with me. I'm looking forward to proofing the piece on sham feeding and truncal vagotomy on conscious dogs by a team of Yugoslavian doctors. Camillia said she couldn't bear to read it, too gruesome. Then I make plans to bump into Wanda. Somebody's got to take care of my pets and Mom's raven while I'm gone, and she's becoming more than my best friend.

Wanda's not listed in the phone book. I'm beginning to wonder if that's her real name. Maybe she has a common real name that she changed for entertainment purposes. Something like Pam Smith. It would be hard to get worse than Pam Smith. There are five Pam Smiths listed and seven P. Smiths. Girls use first initials so perverts who look through phone books for girls' names won't call them up.

The receptionist finally gives me Wanda's home number when I tell him it's an emergency. Wanda says she'd be delighted, I swear, she used the word delighted and when I offer to pay her, just to test her character, she says it's out of the question. I'm feeling really generous. Everything's going my way. The receptionist showed trust in mankind and gave me her number and now Wanda's offered to look after my pets for free. I offer to take her to dinner, but I can tell she doesn't want to take advantage of me, she says No, just leave the keys and instructions, I like that she wants instructions, with her doorman.

I'm sure Wanda's her real name, but I'll find out soon enough.

~

On the train to Louisiana I take two good books. *Moby Dick*, we were not forced to read it in high school, and a true crime book about an unappealing woman in Florida who seduces men and lures them to their deaths. And my veterinary supplies. You never know.

I'm only partway through *Moby Dick* but now Queequeg and Ishmael are already sharing a bed. Didn't anybody back then think that was weird? And for a book about a whale, you sure have to go through a lot of human experience. What a ripoff. I'd rather copyedit the sham feeding piece with dogs. There's no filler. It's concise, and focused on dogs. The best part—it's all true.

Why is it that just when you get to the good part, some fat woman gets on at Philadelphia and stands over your seat breathing heavily while she's putting a suitcase and shopping bags overhead? The whole time she's grunting and talking to something with her called Hermie who has several variations on his name.

Hermie Precious.
Hermie Sweetie.
Hermie Poo.

Mommie's Little Hermie.

Hermiekins.

When she sits down she pushes back the armrest between us and her thighs ooze over onto my seat.

"Excuse me," I smile politely.

"Yes?" she glares at me.

I point to the armrest and start to pull it back down.

"That thing takes up too much room," she says and shoves it back.

"Isn't that so, Hermie?"

"Hermie" pokes his head out of her bag, which is pink vinyl.

His eyes are runny and sort of sad. A Shih Tzu. The kind of dog that compels women to put its hair up in a bow.

You'd think getting to sit next to a dog would make the trip tolerable. I don't have anything against small dogs. I love poodles, pugs, Jack Russells and dachshunds. But Shih Tzus rub me the wrong way. They seem like mascots for defective people and losers. Something about them makes me want to do experiments on them.

She probably feeds him table scraps. Lard, croutons, bacon bits, Vienna sausages, fried chicken in a basket, coleslaw.

I bet Hermie never truly sleeps. He probably has to be constantly aware that at any moment Moby Dick Woman will sit on him, roll over on him or step on him. The constant stress is probably what makes his eyes run. I bet he has an ulcer.

For someone as sensitive to animal pain as I am, this is excruciating. I start to get a tingling feeling when the fat lady and Hermie get up to go to the club car. I could prepare something for little Hermie that would make him forget his troubles for good. I think about this for a few minutes, and wonder if it's really ethical to interfere. I'd like a sign, any sign. When you're not absolutely positive you should do something, if there's any doubt, it's best to wait. Wait for the animal to signal you. Wait for something symbolic. Like if someone shouts "Yes" or "Do it" on the train in the next five seconds, I'd say that's a pretty clear message that I'm on the right track. I'm very attuned to subliminal messages, the kinds of things so many people block out or just plain ignore.

I'm gifted with a logical mind but my logic—and I'm grateful for this—isn't stilted. I take a deep breath and open *Moby Dick* again. I figure out a system. If they don't see a whale by Chapter 30, Hermie will kiss his suffering good-bye.

I read quickly but every time I look up from my book I see the runny-eyed little wretch, so I start to skip parts. Chapter 22, "Merry Christmas." By 25, "Knights and Squires," still no whale. Moby Dick Woman grunts and squeezes out of her seat. She takes Hermie with her, tucked under her corpulent arm so his runny nose is jammed into her armpit. Hermie turns to look at me with a "Help me" expression in his eyes and ducks inside the bag. This is definitely a stroke of luck. I fill a syringe with Tanax and put it in the magazine in the pocket of my seat. Moby Dick Woman comes back with a cheeseburger, which she and "good little Hermie" share.

Ahab shows up by Chapter 27. Moby Dick Woman is wiping ketchup off Hermie's face. Chapter 29. Moby Dick Woman noisily crumbles the hamburger wrappings while Ahab tosses his lighted pipe into the sea. She belches without even putting her hand up to her mouth or turning her head away from me and a horrible rancid hamburger odor spews out. The heck with the whale and illogical superstitions. As soon as she gets up to throw out the trash, the Tanax comes out. How long is she going to hold that garbage in her lap, anyway? I'm sure she'd throw it out the window if it could be opened. As we approach Baltimore she gets up. I pull the magazine out of the pocket and Hermie looks at me with something like hope flickering in his dripping eyes. She puts Hermie on the seat and reaches up for her bags. She's getting off, I realize. I have to act fast. She's not looking at Hermie but she's talking to him as I hold out my hand and whisper his name. We go through a tunnel and the lights flicker. I pull out the syringe and, holding the magazine over it, pull little Hermie over to me. I wasn't counting on him being this maladjusted, deranged, in fact, from life with Moby Dick Woman, because before I can insert the needle into his neck the wretched little thing yelps and bites my hand.

"Your dog just bit my hand," I tell the woman, extending my wounded finger.

"No he didn't," she says. "You monster," and, huffing, she scoops up Hermie and scuttles off with her bags.

My stomach is in knots. In fact, I'm sure I'm getting an ulcer or something after this, but I keep reading. By Chapter 31 they've sighted a whale. Hermie will spend the rest of his drooling days with that woman. I feel like a failure.

But as soon as I get off the train my shoulders relax. The air smells balmy and weedy and mildewed and everything's above ground. New York is so dirty and stressful and all those foul sunless subways I have to take, the only redeeming feature down there is the wildlife, the tiny soot-colored mice, and they try to take even that pleasurable distraction away from passengers by putting out poison.

~

The rooms in the mansion where I'm staying are way too colorful. The bedroom is yellow, sort of a mental illness yellow, like sunflowers. The sitting room is powder blue and the bathroom is what the mansion owners call "blush." If you're not going to jazz up the place with pictures, I say you should go for white. Pure white. But this couple is from Connecticut, where they have a fondness for cozy sweet colors. Maybe they lightened up their New England shades to seem southern. Except for that annoying yellow. I feel like they're trying to alter my moods, get me to relax or something. That must be it. The colors are supposed to be vacation colors—the blue and blush are supposed to be soothing, and yellow is happy—but they just make me want to drink.

I don't know what compels me to do it, I think it's the yellow walls, it's that emotionally disturbed altruistic

Vincent van Gogh yellow. He was an Aries, not logical like a Virgo, but the color still gets to me. So when I leave the mansion, I take my veterinary supplies. I go to Uglishe's for lunch, though the owners of the mansion warn me it's in a seedy neighborhood. I order the crayfish étouffée and sit down at a Formica table. Shoes grate on the concrete floors, scraping chicken bones and grinding spilled sugar. Businessmen are drinking root beer and businesswomen are sitting with their legs crossed. I know these types. They do their drinking at night. At night they drink scotch on the rocks and gin and the ladies, they drink mint juleps.

Mom drank mint juleps.

I drink beer. Dixie. I drink three, in fact.

I feel good when I leave Uglishe's but it's layered over a flat dullness. That hospital visit is gnawing at me. The bedpan odor of the still rooms with milky pastel walls. Sitting sitting sitting for hours by Mom's bed, getting her this and that, hearing how she wasted her life and couldn't keep Hercules, if only I hadn't ruined her chances for more children. But of course, she'll say, it wasn't my fault, God willed it.

The dullness is suffocating, like being locked in the closet. Bill was fond of doing that to me, "Here's a credit card," he'd say. "Get out or die." Not that I mind learning new skills, and I'm locked in these thoughts, the darkness of them, when a guy whips around the corner. I jerk my head sideways to see what's coming at me and I see it in the vacant lot behind Uglishe's. Stoic and still as Egyptian sculpture is a dog poised on a scrap of folded-up carpet. The dog looks like a toy deer, a demented carnival animal, with eyes wide and ears pointed upward, inflated-looking like the ears on a blow-up toy and textured like frozen crinkle-cut French fries. It's stunning. I walk closer. The dog stares at me with a kindly expression, and rather thoughtfully, as though suffering has increased its intelligence. It has sores, open sores, raw and discolored and swollen around the edges. Most amazing of all, beautiful in a weird way, the thing has no fur. The dog is an astonishing Bazooka bubblegum pink.

One of my first thoughts is to call the Animal Rescue. First instincts, though, are something to reconsider. Often they're a thoughtless impulse, a socialized reaction that has nothing to do with true feelings and humanity.

How long would it take the Animal Rescue to get there? A lot of sick people work there. How long would they make the dog wait in a piss-filled kennel to be exterminated? Or would they subject it to the vain and painful process of trying to heal its hopeless mange and disease?

The dog pleads with me with its big gentle eyes, its pupils expanded with pain. I know what he's instructing me to do. And I would do it. I was looking forward to it. The tension builds up until it's almost unbearable and I take out my supplies. The pink dog looks lovingly at me and licks my hand as I fill my syringe with a blend of Fatal Plus and Tanax—my own recipe—which I manage to do skillfully with one hand while the dog showers me with gratitude. They're both effective products, the narcotics soothe the paralyzing effect so it's painless for the animal, maybe even pleasant. The dog tilts his head to one side, the way animals do when they try to look adorable, maybe it's having second thoughts about this, but I am resolute, unwavering in my mission. I am unflinching in my aim at the dog's heart, and with a swift maneuver, I perform the ultimate act of human kindness.

I'm elated, breathing too hard. My pants, my shirt, everything feels too tight. I could rip all my clothes off, which is a startling thing for a restrained Virgo to even think about. I feel ready for anything, even the hospital.

I went to the animal fair,

the birds and the beasts were there,

the old baboon by the light of the moon,

was combing his auburn hair.

Holy Cross Hospital is within walking distance when you feel this good.

I compose a postcard in my head to Wanda.

Dear Wanda,

Mardi Gras beads sparkle like colored tears of mercy. Sequins blown into corners and scattered over the ground glitter like hope.

I've done something important.

See you soon.

Warmest wishes, Pluto

No, better change that to *Cordially.* Yeah. I'll be cordial. I don't want her to think I'm too gushy.

I walk through my old neighborhood and memories stir.

Judy Baker, the redhead from my childhood, wanted a

black kitten in the worst way. Mimi Laroux, she claimed, got a dog by praying at the grotto. I told her I'd heard to get a black cat, you had to get help from the voodoo queen, Marie Leveau. We agreed not to take any chances. We'd do both.

We crossed Basin Street and went to the Lourdes Grotto. The pale blue Madonna with roses on her feet posed passively over rows of candles in blue glass cups. We bought two candles with our ice cream money in the Saint Jude gift shop and took them in. The Madonna looked ineffectual. I thought the statue of Joan of Arc looked like a better bet. She looked tougher. The walls swooned with charred *thank-you*s, *mercie*s and *graciase*s engraved on rectangles and hearts of marble.

I remember asking Judy if she'd make a thank-you and cement it to the wall.

"For a cat?" Judy said. "Mimi got her dog this way."

"Did Mimi make a thank-you?" I asked.

"I don't think so," Judy said. She stood on her toes and dropped her candle into a holder and I thought about setting her hair on fire but somehow it didn't seem appropriate.

For my candle, I chose a spot not near the others. "What kind of dog?"

"A poodle, what else," Judy said.

The light burned harshly bright when we left the grotto and I felt I'd done something dark and evil, lighting a little fire when I wasn't even Catholic. I'd wished for something too. A litter of kittens and a dissection kit.

Then we went into the Saint Louis II cemetery, the second place we wished. Past the tomb of Victor Armant, Delarue, Deflechier, past the baby grave, as we called it, Baby Gladys Schwab died April 26, 1934, age 8 years. Baby Wild died February 17, 1936, Baby Joseph Wild April 23, 1938. How did they look now, their baby bones neatly stretched out, arms folded, Gladys in a rotted ruffled dress and Joseph Wild in threadbare miniature suspenders? Did they have little pets, maybe buried with them?

"Stay to the arrows on the path," I told Judy but I wanted to stray into the narrow spaces between the moldering mausoleums. You could find bones in them, and squirrel nests. It was comforting to be in the cemetery sheltered by the neglected tombs built too close together like tenement housing. I felt hidden and protected. Everything was still and the rabid coil in me would be still, too. Except when I did stuff with squirrels, which was rare, because actually, I only found a squirrel nest once.

Leveau's tomb was gussied up with odds and ends from other wishers. A Colt 45 can with a dandelion and a daisy, an empty perfume bottle, sugar packets, sauce piquant, chicken bones, broken bead necklaces, broken chalk in an oyster shell, the usual stuff, and candles and a glass eye.

I took the pink barrette out of Judy's hair since she didn't have anything else to leave. She kissed it and put it down near the beer can.

Judy scraped her index finger along the crack of the bricks to get a little goofer dust. Her nails were always so dirty you hardly noticed the difference. Details like this still haunt me. Even as a kid, my nails were clean. Parents should give their kids nail brushes. Schools should hand them out. They should do fingernail inspections.

"If Mimi got a dog," I said, "how come I never see her with it?"

"They found it dead," said Judy. "The paws were found tied together, and its head was stuck on a stick."

She made three x's on the tomb with her dust-encrusted nails. I used the chalk to make my x's. Goofer dust is used in voodoo to confuse people, not make a wish. Besides, chalk is cleaner.

Being here sure brings back memories. How could I have forgotten about that nervous little dog?

After I walk past the projects and the cemetery I go out of my way a little to see if the pet shop's still there. Judy and I used to go to look at iguanas, guinea pigs huddled in a sleeping lump—they were always boring to me—so were gerbils. More interesting were the frantic ferrets, squirrel monkeys, evil woolly monkeys, snakes and parakeets, I always wanted to hold one and feel its heart beating, getting faster maybe, the tighter I squeezed. I wanted to feel the smooth feathers, they make pillows out of bird feathers, and down, the softest of all, until the little heart burst of fear, just before I actually crushed it.

I try not to have this fantasy about Sunshine. That wouldn't be very nice, plus ravens are kind of big to squish with one hand. But I've made a conscious effort to hold on to my imagination, my more naive childlike perspective on life. This quality doesn't come naturally to a Virgo. I try to keep my thoughts on the cutting edge, while trying to see life accurately, critically, and try to change things for the better.

I go into the pet shop. The prettiest thing there, in a sickly kind of way, is the Albino King Snake. A weakish pink and white, it's so blanched of color, pencil thin with glassy pink eyes, it looks like something on its deathbed.

One of the guys who works in the store opens the

cage and puts something in. The snake arches up and turns jerkily to seize a little rocking newborn mouse by its blind eraser-pink head, stretching its mouth wide enough to swallow it whole. The little lump, heart still beating, wriggles in its albino pencil case. It's like watching Channel 13.

This kind of thing is exciting, but sometimes I prefer feeling peaceful. This requires finding a safe place. When I get back to New York I'll take Wanda to my sanctuary, the American Museum of Natural History. I know the scenic paintings are probably in poor taste but they really create an atmosphere. The fake water looks so authentic, murky, with leaves and sticks in it. A lot of detail-oriented people took care of painstaking details to re-create the look of natural habitats and posed the animals realistically. What could possibly go wrong? The animals are already dead.

I steer clear of Bourbon Street, where Mom says Bill has started working at Oyster Johnny selling T-shirts and Hurricanes, which only tourists drink. And Bill. I take Royal Street and stop in the Napoleon to have a shot of Fernet, good for the digestion. I have two. I hope the alcohol content doesn't make me reckless.

When I sign in at the main desk in the lobby at Holy Cross I see there's a list of rules.

No smoking.
No alcohol.
No visitors before 8:00 A.M. or after 8:00 P.M.
No more than 2 people allowed in a patient's room at a single time.
No pets.

Now that's cool. Hospitals are filthy places where viral tubercular air is recycled. Who knows what an animal could pick up in a place like this? They say animals have different immune responses and can't catch a lot of human diseases. But I wonder about that. If we're so dissimilar, why do all that cancer testing on cats, dogs and monkeys? Why try mascara on rabbit eyes and Prozac on rats? A human can catch rabies from a dog, after all.

True evolution of consciousness won't take place until veterinarians treat all mammals, including humans. But it'll never happen. The whole reason people become vets is to exclude humans and focus on their real interest. Animals. I think it's a compassion thing. Vets are fairly sensitive people with a clear-cut sense of mission, one in which humans don't figure.

I have this fantasy where there's this car crash on a highway with a middle-class, overweight family and their pet collie, or maybe it's a Jack Russell. A vet is driving by and when he sees the family scattered all over the road, wedged behind jagged metal and punctured with glass shards, he screeches over to them, runs up to the dog, gives it CPR and drives off.

In the elevator in Holy Cross Hospital an orderly in nauseating hospital green, the pants are tight, I mean, they're really tight, pushes a man in a wheelchair attached to an IV and I get this idea that somebody as sensitive and observant as I am might be able to hear the fluid dripping into his veins if only everybody would stop breathing so hard and coughing those annoying, unnecessary little coughs and shuffling their shoes. The orderly's wearing running shoes. Dirty white running shoes. I can't see how that's hospital regulation. I have this playful fantasy about nailing the tips of his toes to the elevator floor. God, his pants are tight. What's he trying to prove? It's disgusting when men try to draw attention to themselves like this. What's the old guy in the wheelchair thinking? They probably have him doped up. Mom will be attached to an IV and I wonder what's dripping into her. I'm sure there's some Valium in it.

I'm staring up at the lights in the elevator and one is burned out. People are so sloppy and irresponsible. Don't they assign someone to take care of this sort of thing? I mean, this is a hospital. When I get to Mom's floor and smell the slowly decaying flowers I remember I've forgotten to bring her something. All I have is my briefcase of supplies, which could come in handy in a place like this, but it's just an idle thought. I should go down to the gift shop but they'll never have Mom's favorite stuff there. Patchouli. Jasmine oil. She likes musk, too, but the idea of Mom sitting in a chilled room on a cranked-up bed and wearing a sleazy secretion from a sac cut out of a deer's belly doesn't seem very healing. Flowers, I decide, will have to do.

I go back downstairs and buy roses. Personally, I find them ordinary, even a little repulsive. Especially with that resurrection expression, *and on the third day he rose again.*

But moms like that sort of thing. Roses, I mean. It makes them feel special, more special than if you buy them carnations, which are cheap. It's important to make a good impression on mothers when they're in the hospital so they think they did a good job of raising you. Hospitals are where good breeding shows.

They're doing some sort of procedure on Mom

when I get there, so I go to the waiting room. There's not a lot that bothers me but people are actually smoking in there. In a hospital. I can't see how that can be legal. I don't let them know how upsetting this is, or that I think people who smoke in hospitals are so inconsiderate they should be eliminated, after giving them a chance with that patch thing, but real smokers would never go for that. They get some perverse and primitive pleasure out of lighting fires and blowing smoke rings. It makes them feel powerful to pollute other people's hair and clothes with their carcinogenic secondhand smoke. And nothing makes them happier than to drive—they like to be the one driving, they have to be in charge—and smoke with the windows rolled up so they can damage the delicate lungs of children. I smile and peruse the magazines until I find something good, the *National Enquirer*, and take it into the hall.

I find an article by Billy Graham. *How to Help Children Learn to Cope with the Death of a Loved One.*

Great, I'm thinking, just what I need to read while Mom's in the hospital. I read it anyway. It looks more interesting than the Elvis found living in the Amazon story, or the piece on giants.

"When I was growing up on a farm, death was an

ever-present reality," says the article. "The animals gave birth and some died. Death was not a secret."

But the line that speaks to me, the line with a powerful ring, is, "In fact, pets are a very good way of teaching children about death."

In the same issue there's a great photo of a chimp, a really cute one, and I could rip it out but I don't. Somehow that would be mean-spirited. It's the kind of photo that could comfort someone visiting family in the hospital. Besides, it's on that cheap sort of paper that wrinkles up when you glue it on the wall.

I hear the metal rings scraping over the rod, a crass sound really, like an alarm clock, signaling the temporary moments of privacy you have in a hospital. They've opened Mom's curtain.

A nurse is still there when I go in. Mom's bed is by the window and she's staring out with a glazed expression like she's not seeing anything at all. I stand by the foot of her bed.

"You have a handsome visitor," says the nurse, pretending to talk to Mom but she's really saying it to me. She smiles and I can tell she's hoping I'll ask her to have a drink after work, or do something to her in the broom closet. I know what these nurses are like, they're just like airline hostesses. Proper, efficient, ingratiating and professional during their day jobs. Sleazebags at night. She disgusts me. The way her body is busting out of the uniform, all that extra subcutaneous fat pressed under that uniform that's a little too small. Why is everyone wearing their uniforms too small around here? I wonder if she'd want to do it in a locked drug-supply closet. Sometimes you have to make sacrifices when you have an ideal.

The nurse puts her hand on her bulging mass of a hip, then fluffs Mom's pillows, again for my benefit. She wants to show off how considerate she is.

"Thank you," I say. I smile in a real nice kind of way, like I think she's a really nice girl, a girl going out of her way to be comforting. Then I consider doing something uninhibited. Why not, I'm thinking, make the right impression. Why not be the kind of man she's wishing for. Charming, confident and sensuous. And subtle, of course. I think about my favorite handsome actors. Gregory Peck. He's just about perfect. But too serious, for this situation, anyway. James Stewart. Too stumbling and awkward. Bogart? He was cool but a thug. What the hell. I throw caution to the wind, look straight at the nurse and I wink.

Then, being the correct person that I am, I go to

Mom's side and embrace her gently, dramatically, kneeling at her side the way people do when someone's dying in a movie.

I look into her eyes and think about the kind of expression Gandhi or Albert Schweitzer or Mother Teresa would have embracing someone they want to heal, and kiss her cool cheek. I let the nurse see this expression so she'll realize that although I have animal desires—I conveyed this with my wink—I am also a loving and trustworthy person, a devoted son.

Mom has this look like she's just waking up.

"Pluto, honey. Can it really be you? How is Sunshine? Did you bring pictures?

"Sunshine's fine. "

"They're going to cut off my foot, the doctor said they have to cut it off."

"Oh Mom," I say. "I'm sorry. Which one?"

"What difference does it make, which one, who wants a woman with one foot? I want to die. I want this to be over."

"At least it's not your kidneys this time," I say. "The kidneys are more serious."

Mom grips the bedrail and lurches up. "They want to cut off my foot. Cut through the bone and chop it off.

Can't you see how horrible that is? I can't go on living. I want to die. I'm going to kill myself. That's what I've decided. I'm going to kill myself."

"Sure, Mom, but in the meantime, how about a grilled-cheese sandwich?"

I know cheese is mucous-producing, and white bread is garbage, but Mom said more comfort could be found in junk food than in tofu and wheatgrass if you had the right spiritual attitude.

"Grilled cheese and ham, my dear heart," she says and clicks on the TV.

"By the way," she says, without looking at me. "Thank you for the flowers. It was so thoughtful of you. Put them by the window."

The nurse comes in and looks at Mom's chart and I ask her if she can get Mom the sandwich.

"Ordinarily, no, I'm not supposed to," she says. "But for your mom, anything."

I bend over and kiss Mom's cheek again and tuck a few strands of matted pale blonde hair behind her ears. She hasn't washed it for weeks. I should ask the nurse to take care of it.

"Mom," I say as I turn to leave, "why don't I ask the nurse to give you a shampoo?"

"Why bother, honey pie? I won't be around much longer." She smiles.

"Mom, you've been saying that since I was twelve."

"It's something I've always known, Pluto. Never mind with the shampoo."

If they were going to give Mom an open coffin she'd want the shampoo. Not to mention a shroud. A woman always wants a new dress. If I were to bring this up she'd say, Why, Pluto, I hadn't thought of that. What will I wear? My paisley caftan? No. I'm sick of it. The Moroccan gown? God, it's so garish. I don't have a thing to wear!

"Let me get you something to cheer you up," I say, and I promise Mom I'll look for a new dress, a coming-home dress, while I'm in New Orleans, maybe something by a designer. Mom immediately suggests this guy she's heard of, Oscar de la Renta, and tells me to use Bill's Visa card. I don't use credit cards. I pay cash. Then there's no record of where you've been, whether it's the vet's or a train ticket. A credit card's like a fingerprint. Not the kind of thing you want to leave all over.

"What color do you think looks best on me?" Mom says.

"Pink," I say, "has always been your color."

The nurse is standing conveniently outside Mom's door when I leave. From the way she's looking at me— she's rapidly moving her eyes from my mouth to my crotch—I can tell she's definitely interested.

"Your mother's an absolute doll," lies the nurse.

"I can imagine," I say. "A southern hippie voodoo doll."

The nurse giggles, then looks puzzled.

I better not get weird on her. If you're too weird, they clam up. Not that I think I'm weird. But I'll keep my creative musings to myself. She's not intelligent enough to get my brand of humor. Wanda would understand. She's not a slut.

I give the nurse my most charming smile. She does have red hair after all, pinned up and restrained.

"How come I never met any girls like you when I lived here?" I say.

She fingers the top few buttons on her uniform. I can see through it, and see that she's wearing something dark under a white slip. As the buttons open I see black straps. This is supposed to be sexy, I guess, but when I see her flabby cleavage pushing out of the dirty slip, the edges yellowed, I start to feel queasy, and get a sinking feeling. It makes me angry that she could be so disgusting. Yes, anger is the correct emotion here. Anger that she has the nerve to think she's being seductive and that I'm letting her make me feel weak.

"What's your name?"

"Edith," she says.

No wonder she's such scum. She's trying to overcome a middle-aged, frumpy name like Edith by sleazing herself up. I hate her name. I hate the way she's dealt with it.

"Gosh, it's charming. Kind of quaint," I say.

"Really? I think it's pretty square. My friends call me Edie."

She doesn't ask me what my name is.

Six buttons are undone now. What does she think? That we'll do it right in the hall near the red plastic bags of human waste material?

I'd like to talk about things that count. Historical things like the death rate in New Orleans during the yellow fever epidemic in 1853. New Orleans had the highest death rate in the country. Or the excavation in the fifties for a new hotel in the French Quarter, the one where bulldozers dug up human skulls and it turned out to be an old cemetery. Or scientific things. You'd think a nurse would be interested in science. Or basketball.

Makes me wonder why they call making it with a girl "scoring," like it takes some sort of skill.

She pulls me, not by the hand but by the belt, down the hall past a tall sealed window. I have this impulse to push her through it but I bet it's the kind of glass that's hard to break. We turn a corner and she takes a key off her belt and unlocks what looks like a closet with a tall cabinet inside, with a metal lock. I guess she's not the talking type.

Bingo. This must be it. It seems worth it now. I feel excited to be in such close proximity to all these substances. One of the small keys dangling from her belt must open this cabinet.

"Edith," I whisper into her ear. The edges of her stingy mouth are brown from smoking. "Unbutton everything." Girls like you to tell them what to do.

She closes the door with a shove of her hip. She unbuttons her uniform and lets it slip over her hips and thighs to the floor like she thinks she's a hot number in a soap opera. The slip, I notice, is held together in strategic places with safety pins but it looks like nylon. I'm sure it's strong enough to tie somebody up with, or gag them.

Not that I'd do anything like that. But I don't believe in inhibiting thoughts. Ideas come to you for reasons.

Subconscious thoughts surface, then seep back in, drip in until they're like frozen ideas waiting to melt.

The slip is strangled around her fat ankle. She reaches for my belt. My excitement has nothing to do with her. I'm excited in spite of her. The idea of her touching me makes me feel limp.

"Take off your shoes," I command and like an obedient dog, she does.

"Slip," I bark.

As she pulls it over her head—she's too fat to pull it down over her hips, I was counting on this—I grab the keys off the floor and slip them into my pocket.

I grab her arms and push her against the cabinet to stall for time, and she moans. Her fingers click against a bulb dangling from the ceiling—you'd think a hospital could get decent light fixtures—and it's swinging, the chain clinking against the bulb. Then I see her five-o'clock shadow armpits. There's a white crust dried over the bristle and I imagine her roll-on deodorant left open— the lid's probably in a dust ball on the floor next to the toothpaste cap.

I never want to see Wanda's armpits. Wanda will stay immaculate to me. Perfect. Kind. Understanding. No wayward hairs. In fact, hair will not be an issue at all.

The corners of her mouth are not browned by cigarettes. And she would never let a stranger humiliate her in a closet.

The keys press against me in my pocket as I lean into her. Her eyelids are greasy, eye shadow caked in the creases like a man-made vein. I think about the keys, like the keys to a brighter future, corny as that sounds. I think about the pink dog, the way it communicated with me, and the tortured animals at the Coney Island Petting Zoo and these thoughts reinstate my mission. I hold my breath and I kiss her.

She's got these teeth, they just bang into you, and she shoves her tongue into my mouth like a medieval serpent, like she's trying to poison me with venom. I'll probably catch a disease from her—human saliva is disgusting. It's too much for me. For Christ's sake, I'm only human.

Think of the animals, says my conscience. But I'm starting to feel incredibly dizzy as she slithers her tongue around and I'm getting a cottony feeling in my mouth, it feels like a color, like the yellow of armpit sweat stains and the swinging yellow bulb, and it glazes over me like goopy French sauce over runny eggs, the eggy, yellow way you feel before you get sick.

A lot of books say Virgos are the hypochondriacs of the zodiac, especially the men. But it's an astrological mis-understanding. Another sign, less meticulous, less aware of the importance of health, the kind of sign that prob-ably disregards subtle as well as severe symptoms with a devil-may-care attitude and finds fault with anyone who is the least bit observant or concerned with their body, is the type to make this kind of accusation. I check my tongue every morning to see if it's coated, and check the color, and take my basal pulse rate as a matter of course. I'm not obsessed or anything. I don't even check my blood pressure. I check these physical aspects the way anyone else might casually inspect a plant for signs of new growth or check to see if it needs water. The only reason I write down my findings is to keep accurate records. That's another thing that's always bothered me about what they say about Virgos. Anal. Virgos simply realize that the human memory is not foolproof.

Stress, like being crammed in a closet with a girl, can bring about physical symptoms.

I squeeze the fleshy web between her thumb and

index finger and imagine that it's the weasel. I imagine pounding a nail through it, nailing her hand to the cabinet. It's metal, maybe the wall would be better. The eggy feeling subsides a little. The weasel would give off a scent, a skunky fragrance like urine and frankincense, a physical spiritual smell, because she's terrified. I've never allowed myself to think about this in so much detail before.

I squeeze the web harder.

"Is that an erogenous zone?" she asks.

"I think it might be," I say. I want to add, "for a weasel," but I don't. She'd think I wanted to have sex with animals or something. People really do that sort of thing. Farm kids and inbred people in the hills. People with severe emotional disorders. Twisted people who confuse physical pleasure with assault and abuse. Think of the diseases that were introduced to humans from all this animal abuse. Serves humans right. If someone's into animals, why can't they get their kicks watching an animal eat another animal? It might be a little unsettling, but there's nothing unnatural about it. And scientific things, dissection, dismemberment, that's cool too. But even science has its drawbacks.

"You have beautiful hands," I tell the nurse as I squeeze the webs between each finger. She's breathing hard, like something exciting is going on. Think fast, I tell myself, what are men supposed to say? Something about her, women like to hear about themselves.

Her bra is still on, thank God, though one strap looks like it would fall down if I loosened my grip on her wrists. If I can only keep her from kissing me again I'll be okay. But she's so strong. It's like she's letting me hold her wrists together because she likes it. I think she'd like it if I tied her up to the bulb, except it looks like it might rip out of the ceiling. All I need is to unlock the cabinet and find a few good tranquilizers.

How much, I wonder, would it take to knock her out? Nurses, most of them I bet, are all junkies anyway. It's one of the perks of the profession. It's probably one of the reasons these girls go into the field, in addition to not being pretty enough to be airline hostesses. Cleaning bedpans, giving enemas. Even if a nurse weren't the junkie type this kind of work could make you want to numb yourself or look for cheap thrills. Then I realize that's all I am to her. A thrill.

I feel used. She has no idea of the kind of person I am. The great ideas I have. My artistic temperament and my mission in life. I'm a piece of meat to her.

She leans toward me, so close I could bite her, tear a

chunk of her selfish flesh out of her fat selfish neck. A dog would do it. A dog would smell her selfishness and growl, a little warning is only fair, and then he'd go for the neck. The dog idea is inspiring. But she'd scream. And my toothmarks would be left as evidence.

Then I remember that I have the keys. I don't need to hang out with the nurse. I can come back anytime she doesn't have a shift. I feel incredibly generous.

"Thank you for a wonderful time, Edith," I whisper, letting my lips brush her ear. "I can't think of when I've had a better time in a hospital."

She looks insulted. I'd go so far as to say she looks wounded.

"What?" she says. "What are you doing? You're not leaving? Leaving me like this?"

"I don't want our relationship to start on the wrong foot," I say, a joke Mom may be able to use pretty soon. I smile sincerely, which is easy since I have the keys and my clothes are on and I can leave at any moment. "A girl like you is a rare gem and I don't want to tarnish your sparkle with a hasty act."

It's important to make a gracious and dramatic exit so the girl feels something great and inexplicable has just happened and so she doesn't look for the keys right away.

I bring her hands down to my face and they're white, like all the blood's run out of them, like Michael Jackson's. Like the true gentleman I am, I kiss one and turn quickly. Then I remember to remind her to bring Mom the grilled-cheese sandwich before closing the door assertively but gently behind me.

There's nothing like triumph to help a guy lighten up. As I take the elevator down, the burned-out light doesn't bother me anymore. It seems a trivial thing, in view of the big picture. A male nurse in tight green looks downright cute. And so what if the tiles are dirty? It's not like they're doing surgery in the elevator. I get too obsessed with details. The keys are in my pocket and all I suffered, really, was a long kiss and I can rinse my mouth with a mild solution of hydrogen peroxide when I get back to the mansion. Just the same, my mouth tastes pretty bad so I gather a lot of saliva and spit—I make sure no one's watching, I know all about bad manners—into the bushes as soon as I get past the hospital entrance.

I stop in the Woolworth's in the French Quarter and pick up the hydrogen peroxide. It's always in an ugly brown plastic bottle. Why can't they bottle it in emerald-green glass like red wine? That would protect it from light just as well. Or anthracite-colored glass, the kind cheap

Spanish champagne comes in. Hydrogen peroxide does sort of sparkle. It gets frothy when you put it on a cut.

I decide to take the streetcar. I don't see one coming so I walk for a while to get away from all the people, past the neurotically condensed buildings, until I get to a long stretch of green. The trolley tracks make me remember how I used to find things that didn't make it across. They'd be in different states of decomposition and there were these tiny red-orange bugs, especially on the birds, in the eyes mostly, and the mouth. There were flies, too, but they were boring, though maggots had that cool wiggle. I was always looking down at the tracks and near the stones—sometimes an animal got thrown a foot or so—and I don't think I ever noticed how beautiful the tracks are, they way they stretch out like bands of tarnished silver polished by late-day sun until they're almost that red-orange tiny bug color and I swear, staring at the tracks I hear a sound, a shrill metallic sound that I'm not sure if it's inside me or vibrating in the tracks. This sound gives me a throb that's centered in my lower abdomen like a part of me's fallen out like a bad tooth. I keep going over to that empty spot and each time I'm surprised it's empty, empty and endless. I hear the streetcar bell in the distance, but there's a cab stopped at the light and I hail it.

I plan one last visit to Mom before I leave on the 3:43 P.M. train to New York. I play around with the idea of having someone come in to give her a pedicure.

After our visit, when I promise to find something exotic for her in New York, I slip out of Mom's room and head down the hall to the closet. No one's around, so I casually put on a pair of surgical gloves—I know I'm probably being paranoid—and unlock and shut the door behind me. I get a kick out of this, feeling my heart beat too fast as if I'm doing something wrong. I try three keys before I find the one that opens the cabinet.

I don't take everything. But I do just about fill my briefcase, I don't want to be greedy, but the plans I have incubating require substantial supplies. Then I lock it and shove the keys under the cabinet like somebody dropped them. When I take off the gloves, my hands are dusted with white powder so they have an otherworldly paleness that makes me think of Michael Jackson again. What is that guy's problem? What sign is he, anyway? Some selfish earth sign. As far as I know he's never done a single decent thing for animals, he exploits them, actually, in his so-called zoo, even if he did name that chimp Bubbles, to give tours to terminally ill kids. Whenever I start to get sucked in by kids, how cute they can be—rare, but it does happen—I make myself remember that they'll grow up in no time to be evil adult Homo sapiens.

The train is filled with evil adult Homo sapiens and their evil undisciplined offspring playing pocket video games, crying and running up and down the aisles, which gets so bad I almost consider going into a smoking car. I have rash thoughts but I control them, except that I can't resist tripping a noisy little brat when she runs by for the 500th time.

～

I love coming home to my pets. The weasel is groggy but lopes to the door and nibbles my shoes, the little dear, and Sunshine caws happily and extends her long, efficient, feminine wings a few times like she's waving and they're iridescent black and purple and even bluer than I remember and I extend my arm and she flaps over and curls her big raven feet around my arm and it feels like friendship, maybe even love.

Wanda wouldn't go for roses. I've got to thank her for taking care of my pets. A Water Pik comes to mind but she already has beautiful teeth. She left me a note. It's in blue medium-point Bic, the type of pen they use at the ASPCA, and I'm hoping she didn't steal it. Maybe she buys this type of pen herself. I hope not. I hate blue medium-point. Wanda should use a crow-quill pen, or a fountain pen, or at least a fine-point because she's such a fine person. Maybe she unconsciously slipped the pen into her bag when she signed out at the ASPCA. That must be what happened.

In the note Wanda says Sunshine perched on her shoulder while she was wearing some nice silk shirt and now she wants to know—I'll call her—if dry cleaning is best for silk, or is hand-washing better, cold or hot water. She wants to be sure, too, that the weasel has had her shots. I warned her about rubber. She was wearing a Swatch. She told me not to worry about thanking her, too.

Of course, the fact that she's told me not to thank her means she expects me to. Girls say the opposite of what they mean, especially if they want to ask for something.

I'll find out where she works and surprise her. I'll take her to dinner to a good place that can spell omelette and there's no typos on the menu but we won't sit by a window under the menu where rude people on the street can gawk at us, or by the bathroom, or by a noisy swinging kitchen door. Or I'll take her for a drink. She may not even drink. Her skin is beautiful, almost see-through. Her eyes are see-through, too, like Jell-O. I was never wild about blue eyes. Blue eyes look good on

Siamese cats and Huskies. But they look creepy on humans. Blue-eyed people lack depth. They're not grounded. They even see colors differently, everything's paler. And when people have those really washed-out blue eyes it looks like they stared up at the sky too long and all the color bleached out of them. Worst of all, their emotions are readable. You can see every shameless nuance of pupil dilation and contraction. It's like their emotions are on display, like they're naked and not embarrassed about what they feel. Emotions are personal, not something to flash around like gaudy sequins. But not Wanda. I don't want her in sunglasses. I feel I should make an exception. We complement each other. She's like a muse.

I could glue up her note with my animal pictures. But no, I want something more dignified. Like framing.

I dial Wanda's number. While it's ringing I mark down the call on the pad of paper I keep by the phone especially for phone call records and I see it's the tenth call I've made since I've lived here, including the two calls I made to find the accurate time and weather.

She has an answering machine. They give me the creeps. Someone could play your message back hundreds of times until you start to sound funny, and I hate hearing myself talk because recordings never capture the depth in my voice. Or you could make a mistake. I hang up and write down what I'm going to say on the recording. I read it a few times until it sounds natural and dial her number again.

"This is a message from Pluto Gerome for Wanda Swann," I say. "Hand-wash with cold water and Ivory soap."

Then I pick up Sunshine, who cocks her head and stares at me funny. I put my finger in her beak and I feel powerful. I could, if I wanted to, just jab my hand right through her. "Sunshine," I say, "you were very bad to Wanda." I kiss her on the head, then we take a shower together and celebrate my homecoming with special food, the one with honey and insects.

I've kept the fan off lately, even though ravens seem to like cool climates. Now Sunshine has a new thing. She pecks. Always at the same place on the floor, like she's trying to poke a hole through to the apartment beneath.

A photographer lives there. His name is Bruce. He has short black hair and he wears one of those bandannas like Aunt Jemima and a leather jacket, even in the summer when I first got here, and now with a hooded sweatshirt but he never uses the hood. He gets a lot of deliveries. Packages from film labs, agencies and magazines. Not any cool magazines, though, stuff I would read. He thinks he's cool but if he's so cool, what's he doing in this building? We don't even have a doorman.

He brings a lot of girls home. Models. He drinks better beer than the Budweiser disco couple across the hall from me, Rolling Rock, it's delivered every Saturday, and he plays better music, too. In fact, his music is great. It's jazz.

The girls are all tall and pretty and don't wear makeup. Most of them wear jeans that are a little too big and have those ripped knees. Jazz is what he puts on right about the time I hear the sex sounds. It amazes me that so many of the girls make animal sounds, like wildcats and coyotes. One barked. But I'd say nine out of ten make a catlike sound. Did they read in some sex manual or magazine that this is a turn-on? It's disgusting. Wanda would never make vulgar noises. I bet if she were to do this kind of thing before marriage, she wouldn't make a peep. Except to whisper, "Pluto, darling."

Maybe Sunshine's trying to peck through the floor because she's homesick for jazz. Mixed in with Cat Stevens, John Mayall and Joni Mitchell, Mom played

Charles Mingus, Miles Davis and Pharaoh Sanders. Jazz was always around in New Orleans. And since my record player has been converted to make art I decide to do something thoughtful for Sunshine. I wait until Bruce leaves on Friday night and I go to the exact spot where Sunshine's been pecking and I drill a hole with the super's drill, telling him I need it to repair something myself, a super will lend you anything to get out of doing any repair work. Now Sunshine will be able to hear the jazz better.

It's too dark to see what's down there so I'll have to wait until Bruce comes home. I put my throw rug, a bearskin with a fake tongue that's getting a little loose but is in pretty good condition otherwise, over the hole so he won't see light coming from my room. Even the lava lamp could give me away.

At 3:09 A.M. he gets home. I'm a light sleeper and I wake up when he slams his door and puts on John Coltrane. That means some girl is with him, the kind of girl who stays out drinking at bars. I don't drink at bars, I'd rather drink in the privacy of my own home. My light's out so I peel back the rug and look into Bruce's place right over the bed. He has black sheets, probably so he hardly ever has to wash them, and the girl is massaging his shoulders. Beer stains won't show up either, good thing, too, because they're drinking beer on the bed. He probably eats in bed, too. She pulls off his T-shirt. He has well-developed deltoids and biceps, a lot like mine.

I wonder if Wanda came into my bedroom. Maybe she sat on my bed. She would have noticed how smoothly my bed is made, not a wrinkle showing through the bedspread, and if she'd lifted up the spread, which of course she would never do, but you never really know with girls, she would have seen that I use hospital corners on my sheets. I'm surprised Wanda didn't at least say something about my decor in her note, not even that she liked my lava lamp, but I guess she didn't think it would be polite.

The girl downstairs unbuckles Bruce's belt, the Harley-Davidson belt he always wears. The leather looks gently worn to a soft patina, which gives it a friendly beauty. I have this idea that he softened the belt by strapping girls with it, just to get them to stop howling, but it's more likely he hits them to make them howl. I don't know why everybody and all these girls think fashion photographers are so hot. It's not like they're doing anything so hard. It's wildlife photographers who are underrated. I'm not talking about those guys who take pictures of pedigrees at trade shows and pets at photo salons. I mean the people who crouch for hours on tundra to get a compelling shot of a baby seal. Animals aren't mercenary. They're reluctant, in fact. Dangerous. And they move. You have to travel far to find them, unlike girls, who are a dime a dozen. And for wildlife you need patience.

It's like, you turn on the TV, usually I only watch nature shows, but sometimes I'll get caught up watching a special on runway shows or on some guy, some artist of the fashion world snapping away at a girl on the beach, and the girl is dying to get her picture taken, you can see it in her eyes, she's so cooperative, and she's even getting paid. Nobody pays animals.

Bruce unzips her baggy jeans with his teeth, but that's all. She does the rest. They both drink some more beer and then she gets on top of him. He's saying something, he's mumbling so it's hard to hear exactly, and every time he says it she mews like a cat in heat. It's a real turn-off. He's got his eyes closed—I don't blame him—so she could be any girl, and he's holding on to her gravity-defying grapefruit protuberances. She seems to be doing all of the exercise but he has to put up with all that hair flying around in his face. I go to the kitchen and get a beer and when I come back they're doing it doggie style, an expression that seems like an insult to dogs.

~

I wake up cold in the middle of the night. 4:27 A.M., actually. Sunshine is yelling and my arms are sticking out of the blanket. Three days before Christmas and no heat. And it's Friday. That means no heat until Monday, probably. This is one of the bad things about living in New York. You'd think in a northern climate they'd figure out how to keep a boiler working. What are people with babies supposed to do? And what about animals? Mammals in particular.

As my eyes grow accustomed to the dark—I take vitamin A supplements, good for night vision—I can make out the eyes staring at me from the walls. Livid yellow panther eyes hover over my night table. Next to them I see the roundish lemur eyes, I'm sure it's the lemur because there are smaller eyes right above it, the baby on its back, Siamese cat blues, capuchin monkey eyes, tiny and distant, a group of them in the forest photo, and next to that more golden eyes, probably the fruit bat. Limbs and fur are becoming visible in the dim light and because it's so cold my thinking, considering I just woke up, seems incredibly clear. I see the moist glistening of a long greenish-yellow leg of an exotic tree frog from Brazil. It's kind of haunting in here with all these eyes and damp amphibians and these steady droplets of ideas start to form, dripping on me like some kind of Chinese water torture. I have all these ideas about how I should dedicate my life, but dripping in with these blissful tasks are the drips whispering that I might be misunderstood. Instead of feeling comforted by the animals I feel the thunder of conflicting thoughts pounding in me and as the thoughts hit in rapid succession, each separate and unconnected, I have this second epiphany, that I'm kind of a drip, too, that I have no connections to anyone, not in New York, except maybe for Wanda and I suspect I've inflated my opinion of myself to her in my eyes, like a delusion, so I won't feel so different from everyone. I know I'm different. But if I'm honest with myself, and it's moments like this when truth gets into bed with you, you find out it's not cute, like a little monkey. It's hairless, smooth and very human, and it has bad breath and then you feel even more alone, because even though you want company in bed, it feels all wrong. Like incest.

I can put on wool socks, sweatpants and my bathrobe. It's a smoking jacket, rose with magenta collar and cuffs, in a jacquard pattern, kind of fancy. Very Clark Gable. I think Wanda would think I look smart in it. Even though

I hate the name of it, *smoking jacket*, like smokers would only smoke in the privacy of their own homes. It's the privacy I like about the smoking jacket, the at-home personal feeling it conveys.

But I'm digressing. People in my building are probably waking up and calling the super, he won't answer the phone, and putting on warm clothes. But do they think about their pets? I'll put my down coat over Sunshine's cage. She's not used to winters up here, even though she's a native northerner. Mom would keel over if anything happened to Sunshine. She makes me send her Polaroids every month. I'll give the weasel a wool sock to crawl into. What are other people doing? A lot of people don't realize that they've created an unnatural environment for their pets. There are a few old ladies with little sweaters for their dogs. But most people around here walk their dogs to the store in subzero weather and leave them chained up outside while they shop. No dog in real life is going to just sit there in an unsheltered area and wait. This should be considered a criminal act.

It'll never happen. Some crazy woman was passing out Xerox copies on garish neon paper in the Village to people in coffee shops who left their dogs shivering outside. The note said something like, "How would you like to be tied up outside while your dog came into a warm place to sit down for a while and have a meal? You are a monster. You are inhumane. Clearly, you do not believe animals have rights. You should not be allowed to have an animal."

Nice try, but does she think the type of person who leaves animals tied up outside is concerned with animal rights? These types need animals to boss around. They make their dogs do humiliating tricks. They go away on vacations and leave their animals in a strange kennel where they could pick up fleas. Then they have to dust the dog with flea powder and set off flea bombs and toxify their whole apartment with noxious fumes that seep into all their clothes and towels. Creating awareness doesn't work. You have to take action to make people listen. You have to take drastic measures.

I hear a door in the hall slam so I get out of bed and look through the peephole. It's the disco-playing, Budweiser-drinking couple across from me. They're bundled up and carrying chintzy little nylon suitcases. Probably going to a hotel or to stay with friends, except I doubt they have any friends, they're so unlikable. What do they plan to do with the cats? She hates the cats, they're his. She won't let them in the bedroom. I only know about this because she's so loud. I can hear her yelling at him over the disco that the "goddamned cats don't belong in the bedroom." They're leaving without the cats, I knew it, I knew it. The cats won't even be able to curl up on the comforter, if they have a comforter, so they'll shiver on the vinyl sofa or under the sofa or pace the cold, sticky kitchen tiles, I've never seen their apartment but I can just tell the sofa's Naugahyde. They're probably slobs so the cats will have a sweater left on the floor at least.

I look over the last few entries I made in my diary:

Monday.

Taste buds very pronounced. Deep pink with a white coating like salted red-dyed pistachios. Basal pulse 78.

Tuesday.

Rather pale with a white coating. More like salted cashews. Basal pulse 79.

Wednesday.

A decidedly yellow cast, pronounced bumps, white coating particularly toward the center and back with the look of peach fuzz or baby chick fur. Basal pulse 80.

I'm sure I need more exercise. It's this desk job. And I spend too much time worrying about animals. My health horoscope for December says I should think about health for the masses, and that with my grasp of detail, I can excel in service to others but that I could become exhausted performing these health service tasks. My Pluto is in Virgo in the Eighth House. I don't know why people think the Eighth House is so bad. I'm not vindictive. I'm very moral. Too moral, in fact. It's burdensome to feel so responsible.

I should start walking Wanda home. All I have to do is show up where she works. Where does she work? I'd love to hear her sing or whatever. I'm glad she's not a waitress. I'll get her to tell me. If she won't, which is possible if she's a Pisces, they're so secretive, I can find out. Virgos are good at the details.

Thursday.

Very pale, nearly white, coated. Basal pulse 77.
Drinking detox tea.

Friday.

Faintly rosy. Coated, not as heavily as yesterday.
Basal pulse 76.

Maybe I should start checking Le Sang's tongue every day. She's been sneezing again. A nasal drawn-out squeak. It's not dust. There's no dust in my apartment. It must be another cold. Maybe acupuncture would help. She sure has been getting a lot of colds. I hope she doesn't have weasel immune deficiency. Maybe I should take her to the homeopathic vet downtown. She must have gotten a chill when the heat went off. At least she'll be okay this summer, I don't have air conditioning.

People in New York complain about the heat and humidity all summer. They all use air conditioning. I hate air conditioning. It's so unnatural, and it gives me a cold. It probably fills your lungs with chemical agents. I bet air conditioning even affects your thinking. And it's ugly. Now, a fan is something to look at. It's natural. It spins. It has rhythm.

I had this fantasy recently where Sunshine's staring at the fan. I've tried not to think too much about her, but there's something about the way she seems transfixed by it that makes me feel so creative. It's things that spin, I'm realizing, things that spin that get to me. Like my spin art. I love squirting those violent colors and watching them spin off the paper. There must be something about the blades that makes me lose control of my imagination. These things occur to you when it's not really your own pet, especially if it's not your pet and somebody really loves it and is counting on you to take care of it, or if you haven't had the pet a long time. In real life, Sunshine flies from her dead tree branches in the corner to the end table and stares at the fan on the windowsill. I just complete the picture, so to speak. In my fantasy, she jumps to the edge of the windowsill and hops toward the fan with her wings extended like a tightrope walker. The wind ruffles her feathers, lifting them up a little, and she likes how this feels. She cocks her head and the beady eyes have a glint in them like glass, an evil glint Mom never noticed. She thinks Sunshine has a mournful, remorseful expression, one filled with the memory of great pain because she's the reincarnation of Barabbas, and the glassy eyes follow the movement of the fan. Poor deluded Mom, still clinging to the idea of reincarnation. Why did she leave me spinning in that chair? I hated it. I'd get sick spinning after eating all those peanuts and my hands got oily and salty and it would never wipe off on those stiff cocktail napkins. I hate those napkins. They're so little and scratchy and they're not absorbent. Why do they even bother to make them?

I try to stop the fantasy because it makes me feel so tense, so I try looking through *Animal Kingdom* magazine but I can hear the fan, and every time I look up I see Sunshine staring at it. It isn't in keeping with my philosophy of life, it's so grim, it's Mom's Sunshine, after all. But the fan is unsettling, the way it circulates these memories and Sunshine walks trancelike up to the fan, but not headfirst, I couldn't see the expression that way, but sort of sideways so one wing gets sucked in and iridescent black feathers sparkling with red droplets burst into the room. The blood hits the floor first, then the feathers flutter down. What bugs me most about this fantasy, besides having succumbed to it in the first place, is that I have to see the thing through. I imagine myself getting out the Top Job and cleaning up with a sponge, the pink one I only use for floor spills.

At work we've been on deadline, and everything's behind, because the researchers turned their material in late. How can you trust their research if they can't meet a deadline? So thanks to them, I have to take short lunches at weird times, sometimes no lunch, and it's weeks before I run into Wanda at the ASPCA. Finally on Friday I have time to go and I see her bringing back the Dalmatian with the paralyzed leg. I wonder if it would be better off without the leg altogether. Anyway, I want to invite her to go to Chinatown for the Chinese New Year. She seems a little nervous when I see her again, she keeps shifting her weight so she takes these little steps backwards, maybe that's a sign of shyness.

She's got on soft suede slip-on shoes the color of a wild squirrel and this shirt like a deerskin color or chamois, kind of plain and modest, maybe even a man's shirt, it's a little too big and her delicate clean fingertips dip out of the sleeves like tapering albino kitten tails except they're not furry, so maybe shaved kitten tails would be more precise.

One of the things I like about her is that nothing's loud. And things about her physically don't bother me, either. She's tall, like I am, and there's nothing sticking out or hanging off or bulging or bumpy. She looks . . . decent. Decent girls don't draw attention to themselves. They do things like walk animals on their lunch break and work in music stores and compose symphonies and ballads in the solemn quiet of their apartments and I think they probably get overlooked. Decent girls are the ones men should open doors for but I think most guys notice the girls in sleazy clothes, clothes that are too small and stretched tightly over all their bumps and swells and lumps, girls who look like they're on their way to a disco in the middle of the day. Where do they work to dress that way? I ought to get Wanda something fancy in Chinatown, maybe something not quite so pale and plain, something that lets her know she's a woman, like something in silk with a dragon or a snake.

"You know," I say to Wanda, taking a step away from her so she'll ache to be closer to me, "I was thinking Chinese New Year might be like Mardi Gras. It'll be Mardi Gras soon, early February, and I feel kind of, how do I put it, homesick."

Her face gets this soft strange look like she's watching *Romeo and Juliet*, the scene in the tomb, or *Bambi*, right after his mom gets shot by a hunter. She must be a Pisces.

"And," I say, gazing into the distance with a tragic expression, "you know my mother won't be around . . . much longer."

"I'm so sorry," says Wanda. She stretches out her shaved-kitten-tail fingers and grabs my hand.

"Mom is such an extraordinary woman. I was hoping to buy her a dress in Chinatown. Only I'm not much good at picking these things out, women's things."

"I'll help you," Wanda offers. Her pupils are the size of dimes. If Wanda were any other girl I'd think the idea of shopping was turning her on but with Wanda, I know it's got something to do with her big heart and her reaction to me.

"Tomorrow?" I say.

"Yes, but I work that evening."

"I'll drop you off at work."

"Oh no. You don't have to," she says. "I have to go home and pick up a few things."

"Well, you'll at least let me take you home."

"No, that's okay."

I decide I'll see her home anyway. And then to work. She must be embarrassed about something. Maybe the pay is lousy. Or the place isn't elegant enough. I'm sure it's something she thinks will reflect poorly on her character. I'll prove to her that these things don't matter. I'll be so stealthy, she'll never see me following her.

That night, to prepare for my big date with Wanda tomorrow, I take a bath with Epsom salts to detoxify. We're made for each other. Both of our first names end with vowels and have five letters. I won't shave until tomorrow, though, so my skin is smooth when I kiss her good-bye on the hand or cheek. I wonder if Nair is effective.

Le Sang waggles in and stands up on her hind feet. She has a hard time balancing, sometimes when she wakes up she pulls herself across my bed with her front paws and her back legs have a paraplegic quality I always thought was adorable. She must want to get in the tub.

"Want a bath, little weasel?" I say. I pick her up and she licks water off my hand. I let her tail dangle in the water and she doesn't seem to notice. The tail looks scraggly when the fur is slicked down and I feel like dipping in the little feet, she's got those webs, after all, good for swimming. The weasel doesn't like it. She's scratching me to get out and I realize that it's best if Le Sang has her little swim when I'm not in the tub. She'll learn to like it. I reach over to the rack for a towel, all cotton of course, polyester rejects water, and dry Le Sang off, making sure I dry between each little web. God, I love those little webs, they're so delicate so I just squeeze one a little, I can't help it. When I put her down she fluffs up her fur like some injustice has been done to her and backs out of the room, chirping, like she doesn't trust me.

The Chinese don't have a weasel in their astrology. I make a mental inventory of all the animals and wonder which one Wanda is. I'm a sheep.

I never liked being a sheep. They seem so defenseless. For years I thought they must have gotten the year of my birth wrong, some sloppy slip of the pen. They're so careless in hospitals. You wonder if they get the birth time right, too. I can see it now, some doctor after fifteen hours of labor saying, "Oh, shit, nurse, the birth certificate. What time was that kid born?"

In Chinatown, Wanda and I will have bean curd with snow peas, and fortune cookies, and then I'll ask her what her Chinese sign is. I bet if they checked out the sign of the types of people who bump into you in the subway and don't let you get off the train before they burst in and walk too slowly down narrow supermarket aisles, most of them would be oxen and pigs. Not that I have anything against pigs, they're very intelligent, or have anything against any animal, but anytime you give humans animal qualities it's bound to make the animal look bad.

Wanda's wearing gloves the color of asparagus. We meet at the corner of Canal and Mott where we stop for a minute at a fruit and vegetable stand and her asparagus tips disappear in a heap of snow peas. I buy papayas, good for the digestion, and then we head for Mott Street where Wanda says the dress shops are. We pass a shop selling firecrackers, which are illegal, and I buy seven packages.

Everything in the first shop is so shiny it looks like silk but Wanda says a lot of dresses are made out of rayon, which Wanda says snags easily and pills.

I'm impressed Wanda knows about fabric but I hadn't

expected her to shop like such a regular female. She's sorting through a rack like women do, sizing up every garment with a beady once-over, her eyes sharpened so she's got this expression like Sunshine totally fixated by the fan. Wanda's pulled the asparagus off her hands and she's petting a coral-colored dress.

"Does your mother like coral?" Wanda asks.

"Mom looks good in all colors," I say. "What about you? Do you like coral?"

"I love coral," she says. Then she looks wistful. "But I never actually wear it. It's so cheerful."

"Exactly," I say, resolving to mix more red with yellow in my spin art. I'll do a piece called *Wanda's Hair.* "Exactly why I'm buying it for you."

"Oh, no, Pluto," she says. "We're here for your mother. Besides, it isn't my size. I'm hardly a ten."

She gets a wounded look like I've said she's fat and I realize I'll have to undo this damage poetically.

"Why of course not, I was just looking at the color, Wanda. I didn't think you, a starling-thin sparrow of a girl, would be a size ten. You're a mere slip of wind, as lithe as a feather, so much so that I feel ticklish around you."

Wanda smiles that clean white toothpaste-ad smile and reaches over and tickles me, under my armpits, where thank heavens I've used deodorant, the natural kind. For a second I got carried away, I felt understood but I didn't expect Wanda to do anything so forward. I guess I have no one but myself to blame for her brazen behavior. I shouldn't underestimate the power of my words on my little swan.

I buy two of the coral dresses, one for Mom in a size ten, and one for Wanda in a size six. I hope there's no sick resemblance in my subconscious mind between Wanda and my mom. Wanda would never be desperate enough to run around in transparent pants in a nightclub, for one thing. Wanda kisses me on the cheek, a perfectly acceptable response.

Deeper into Mott Street there's a typically tacky, overdone Chinese arcade. I like it, the painted carved fire dragons and the paper banners and lanterns and dragons being ravaged by the wind. The wind is so aggressive here. It's like a crazy person, doing senseless barbaric acts. I can't relate to it, its reckless temperament, but I can appreciate nature, its uncontrollableness. I just wish it would stop messing up my hair. I have to take a comb out every thirty seconds—I try to do it when Wanda's not looking, I don't want her to think I'm vain, because I'm not, I'm just neat. I kind of like Wanda's hair wind-blown. It makes her look like she's having a good time. We walk under the dragons and Wanda points to a little shop with two chicken-wire cages. For seventy-five cents, you can exploit chickens. One plays tic-tac-toe with you. The other one dances. When it's in the mood. There's a disclaimer above the cage.

This will be the true litmus test of Wanda's character. I'll put in a few quarters and see if she's amused by this barbaric Chinese torture.

"Isn't that horrible," she says. "It dances."

"You've been here?" I ask.

"No, but the idea seems so cruel," she says. "Making an animal dance so we can be amused. And it's so cold out here. The poor thing."

I slip the quarters in and a door slides up. A pure white chicken steps out and pulls a light on. The naked bulb glares, a meager source of heat, and it steps, shuffles really, from side to side like somebody nervous or seasick and then walks back into its cage and the door slides down.

Wanda looks at me like I'm a bug or something. "Why did you do that?" she says.

How can I explain that it's like picking a scab, it's irresistible, I'm not a conceptual person, I want to see things, even sad, horrible things? And just because I might even enjoy them doesn't mean I don't know the difference between right and wrong. And how to deal with it. She has no idea how noble I am, how devoted.

"Maybe we should set it free," I suggest.

"It would freeze out here. A quick death would be kinder," Wanda says, running her asparagus fingers along the wire, which is wide enough to throw in a firecracker or inject something lethal.

"Yes, death is always kinder," I say, knowing that I will eventually become a hero in Wanda's blatantly blue eyes.

I take Wanda to the subway at Canal. "After you," I smile at the turnstile and slip a token in for her.

"What train are you taking?"

"Well, from here, I take the N or the R."

"I take the N or R, too. Just to Twenty-third, then I walk over to Chelsea."

"I live on the East Side. Gramercy Park," offers Wanda.

When we get to Twenty-third I graciously extend my arm before Wanda to indicate that she is to exit the subway car first. We get upstairs and I turn, abruptly, so she doesn't think I like her excessively, after all, I just bought her a dress and I don't want her to think I expect to get something out of it, or that I'm a sugar-daddy type.

"Bye," I wave and walk without turning back. But I only take a few steps before I pause to pretend I'm tying my shoelace to see which street she's taken. She's turning toward Twenty-second. I follow her and wait across the street from her apartment in a coffee shop with tinted glass so I can discreetly observe her. She's bound to leave for work soon. I'll find out where.

A couple leaves. The first thing I see is red, a redhead nestling her head on the shoulder of a big guy and I feel sick, like a blob of lava cold and sunken in the bottom of a lava lamp with a burned-out bulb, but then I see it's not Wanda, it's some tacky girl in white boots, scuffed up like she's never heard of shoe polish, and pants way too tight, she must be an off-duty nurse, and her hair color doesn't even look real. And her face, that's the worst part, looks like a bulldog's, and that just doesn't look good on humans.

Eight minutes go by and I order a fresh orange juice. A fat woman leaves Wanda's building next, it seems hard for her to open the door. She has a pig face and she's walking a dog in February, freezing cold out, with no sweater on it, just a lavender hair bow. It's a little Shih Tzu, of course.

I hardly pay any attention to the next person to leave

because she's blonde. But there's something striking about her. She has the gentle stride of Wanda, her demeanor, her asparagus gloves, but big blonde hair, like Dolly Parton, and big black shiny shoes with a thick sole, and her little legs in black nylons with a seam are disappearing into the black shoes like they're being carried away by big black evil bugs. She seems like a showgirl version of Wanda. If she didn't have on the sunglasses I'd know for sure, it could be her sister or something.

She gets in a cab and I have that empty feeling. I wait another half hour and then check out the building for rear and side entrances. Maybe she called in sick. Lovesick. Or really sick. Maybe the Chinese food got to her. I'm feeling a little queasy. You can never be sure they don't use MSG or sugar. But it might be nerves. I call Wanda from the pay phone. No one answers.

I get to the coffee shop early on the following Saturday and order an orange juice. I call Wanda from the pay phone. Wanda answers, kind of breathlessly.

"Pluto here. I thought you might like to go for a cup of coffee." Not that I really drink coffee. It's bad for the pancreas.

"Thank you very much," Wanda says. "But I'm late for work."

"Another time," I say, and wait for her to leave.

The pig woman leaves. But no one else for at least ten minutes. If Wanda was already late when she spoke, she must have severe afflictions in her astrological chart. Unless I've somehow missed her.

Then I see her again. The Dolly Parton blonde. Sunglasses again. And asparagus gloves. I'm confused, but something tells me I should follow her anyway and I leave two dollars for the juice because I'm a generous person and hail a cab seconds after I see her get in one and say to the driver, "Mohammed"—I know his name because I always memorize the name and cab number when I get into a cab, just a good habit I guess—"follow that cab." I slam the door and then I smell it. Mohammed is smoking with the windows rolled up so I say, pleasantly, which isn't so easy when you're in a hurry, "Hey Mohammed sir, could you please put out your cigarette, please?" Then I add, "allergic" and smile.

Mohammed says no he can't, and I explain that this is illegal and he explains that the Koran says it's fine to smoke. This doesn't work out.

The next driver is Julio, big on air freshener and hair pomade but I stay in his cab anyway.

"See that cab," I say, pointing to the blonde's cab still stopped at a red light. I give him the license number. "Could you follow it, please? It's violently important."

"Violent?" says Julio.

He creeps up to a Volvo like he's considering not taking me as a passenger.

"Not violent, it's just an expression. I mean it's very important."

"Life is not a movie," says Julio, and I can see he's the pseudophilosophical macho type you need to flatter with the basest sort of flattery, of course, because he feels like a loser driving a cab, in his own country he's a neurosurgeon, no, a rock star, so I say, "Julio, forgive me for being so personal but I was just wondering, you look so much like him, are you related to Elvis Presley?"

The light turns green and the car jerks forward.

Julio turns around while he's driving, which makes me very nervous, and smiles at me. "I know what you mean," he says. "Mostly my profile, yes?"

"Well, I did see your profile first, oh, her cab is turning, see, up ahead?"

"Yes, I see it. So not just my profile?"

"I'd say you have Elvis, more distinctive, though, you know what I mean, written all over your face. Don't get too close though, Julio, I don't want her to see me. I want to surprise her."

"Of course. I have the Sun Studio recordings. I'll play them."

"Wow. Great," I say.

"You know, in my country I am a musician."

"I knew it," I say.

"Her hair is very big. Blonde. She is your girlfriend? You are jealous? You had a fight?"

"She's my fiancée," I say and this seems to satisfy Julio.

"So your fiancée, she likes Elvis Presley?"

I realize that I have no idea. I hope not. I hate Elvis, his graphic pelvic thrusts and gyrations and pansy crooning. His hair was greasy and later in life he went for those low-cut white outfits and all those rings, without any real style. At least Liberace had elegance. No fiancée of mine could like Elvis. Wanda would like Mozart, Wagner, Beethoven or good jazz.

"Oh, yes, she adores Elvis," I tell Julio. "And South American music, too."

"I am from South America!" Julio beams and tails the mystery woman just like a cabbie in a movie, pulling over inconspicuously across the street when we see the big-haired blonde woman get out of the cab in front of Les Gals Sauvages, a topless S & M bar. She bends over toward the window and hands over the money in the asparagus gloves, her fingers lengthening like a high note held for a long time. I have a sinking sick feeling they could be Wanda's hands, even though it doesn't make sense. I'll have to find out if she has a relative staying with her. I'm sure that's it. A relative from the wrong side of the tracks.

"Oh my God," I tell Julio. "I've followed the wrong woman. That is definitely not my fiancée."

Risking a cold, I open my window to clear out some of the air-freshener scent and I ask Julio to turn the radio down and take me to West Twenty-second Street. When I get home I take off my shoes at the door so I don't track urban filth into my apartment and turn on the fan to watch the blades spin so I can stop thinking for a while.

After I get dizzy from the fan I turn on the lava lamp and wait for it to warm up. Gradually, the purple blob swells and rises and blobs down in smaller globs. I hate those words, *glob* and *blob*. The lava, I'll just call it lava, is like a melting metaphor, an emotional mirror. It's like I'm watching my insides heat up, the tension building until I expand, rising upward but then, because I'm contained, having to sink back to earth except the inside of the lamp isn't earth, it's someplace I haven't figured out yet.

I get the filter vacuum and suck up the gunk, I hate that word *gunk,* in the gravel in Bacteria's tank. I've got to go to the pet shop and get more goldfish. I'll pick out the plump, pretty ones.

~

By noon I've copyedited and proofed two inspiring articles, my favorite about inducing pancreatitis in mice with injections in the tail vein, I mean, a mouse is so little, I can appreciate these small details, and it revs me up to go to the pet store during my lunch hour. I pick fifteen goldfish, each one slightly different in color, fin size, et cetera and then I find a book on telepathic communication with animals. The cover isn't very dynamic but I guess publishers who end up doing books on animals use only a small portion of their annual budget on design. The paper seems cheap, too.

I read a little of it back at the office. The goldfish in the plastic bag on my desk are staring at me.

"Pluto," says Camillia. "Aren't they cute." Then she adds triumphantly, like I've become a member of an exclusive club, "Now you have your own pets."

"Yes, they are cute," I say.

She stoops down, mainly so I can see her cleavage. She's wearing that red power suit—it always makes her so aggressive—and she doesn't have on a blouse, just a loose scarf, and glares at the fish.

"It always bothered me that they can't blink," she says, which is possibly the most sensitive observation she's ever made.

Animals are underestimated. The author of the book I just got thinks so, too. My favorite part is when the author has a chat with her hamster about letting it loose in the woods to die—it's got a cough, which doesn't sound fatal to me, but anyway, after warning the hamster that a predator will most likely kill it she lets the sickly little thing go, though I wonder why she didn't take it to the vet, these kinds of people are always taking something to the vet, even when the animal isn't their own, they feel responsible on a bigger scale, like I do.

The next morning she has a telepathic flash that the

hamster was killed by a raccoon and as it was being eaten, the spirit of the little thing has this evolved thought as it ascended, that the raccoon was so pretty it wanted to be a raccoon in its next life. Animals respect predators. They understand the intrinsic beauty of things more powerful than they are, animals that can eviscerate them or snap a spine in a single swift motion.

I don't buy everything in this book, like the stuff on reincarnation, but I have always had a special rapport with animals—I can feel what they're thinking—and I'm hoping to communicate better with Sunshine to get her to do things, to be a part of my noble vision.

When I get home I turn on the lava lamp and as it heats up, I have this fantasy where Sunshine carries things in her beak and flies over transoms in my building. She drops things in pet food left out rotting for cats. I would not do anything unethical like make her steal things, even though I know ravens have a natural attraction to shiny objects like diamonds. I would never abuse my relationship with Sunshine in that way.

The Budweiser disco couple is fighting. Animals at least, except maybe for chimps, only fight for a reason. They usually only kill each other for food. The couple is fighting over the cats. The cats they left to freeze when the heat went off. He pays too much attention to them, she argues. More than he does to her. They're ruining her pantyhose, getting fur on her clothes and snagging anything she doesn't put away. The cats are probably trying to discipline her. To get her to clean up her act. I bet he doesn't leave his clothes lying all over the place.

I'm sure all this arguing is traumatic for the cats. They should not have to live with these people, even if their basic biological needs are being met. I think about letting them loose but they wouldn't survive outside, especially since it's winter. There's only one thing to do, which would teach the couple a lesson and save the cats from the constant harm they suffer. They'll never have to listen to that woman's nasal voice again, and they won't have to suffer from the fumes, she has painted nails which means the cats are inhaling nail polish fumes and nail polish remover fumes all the time, not to mention hair spray, I can tell she uses a lot of hair spray and she smokes. They both smoke.

"Sunshine," I say in my most commanding voice, one that Napoleon would have used to address a small animal he loved but dominated, "Sunshine, come here." I extend my arm and Sunshine, bless her little heart, flies right over and perches obediently on my arm.

The phone rings and Sunshine digs her claws into my arm like it's my fault. We both feel our privacy is being violated but I answer the phone like it's the normal thing to do and it's Mom.

"Pluto, unless the feeling in my foot comes back it's coming off next week."

I think about telling Mom not to worry, that some guys are actually into that kind of thing. That I've seen an erotic magazine called *Amputee Love*. They might even have subscriptions.

"Mom," I say, mustering confidence to sound cheerful, "think positive thoughts. I was thinking I could get you a subscription to a needlepoint magazine."

Mom is silent for a long time like she's considering that. I hear a TV in the background. The theme song to "The Addams Family." I always loved watching those reruns.

"Pluto, dear," she says. "I think I should do myself in. Call that doctor who can do it for you."

"Gee. How much does somebody charge to do that?" I ask to put her in touch with practical reality. "And what does Bill think?"

"Bill," says Mom, "asked if you could please return his credit card."

Sunshine caws and I ask Mom if she wants to talk to

her. I put the phone up to Sunshine's ear and she listens attentively and pecks into the receiver a few times.

"Think of Sunshine," I say.

"I do," says Mom. "Every day. I have her pictures up over my bed."

"I hope you didn't put thumbtack holes through them," I say, just to lighten things up.

Mom is dead serious, though. "Oh, no, I used surgical tape."

"You could make a little needlepoint cape with wing slits for Sunshine, you know," I say. "It'll be winter soon and it's much colder up here."

"I hadn't thought of that," Mom says. "Do you think you could send me one of those magazines?"

"Sure, Mom."

"Kisses to Sunshine."

I hang up and resolve to have a great session with Sunshine. I send her a mental image of herself winging over a transom toward a water bowl, with a tiny vial in her right claw, and she opens it and drops it in. Then I give Sunshine a Number 2 pencil, half a pencil actually, and command her to fly across the weasel's water bowl. She doesn't, she just looks at me. So I take the pencil and go over to the bowl and drop it in. Then I give it back to her and she doesn't even want to hold it. So I wrap the pencil in aluminum foil—shine gets to her every time—and after I show her what to do a few more times, I hand Sunshine the pencil and command her to fly to the bowl and she does.

Then I reward her with an M&M, the kind with peanuts, even though it has sugar in it, because the reward system has to be compelling.

We practice until Sunshine's had ten successful drops. I take a Polaroid of Sunshine holding the pencil and then I write Mom a note.

Dear Mom:

Your beautiful, darling, brilliant Sunshine now delights in performing tasks. She even brings me my pencils. She's in excellent health, of course. She's got a Virgo looking after her! I feel she's destined to do great things.

Love, Pluto

P.S. Your needlepoint magazine is on its way.

I hear Bruce slam the door downstairs. He doesn't have pets. Just those girls. He goes away sometimes for weeks at a time, so it's a good thing he doesn't have any pets. They'd just die, unless I slipped food to them from

Sunshine's music-listening hole in the floor. He leaves with a lot of equipment, I see him in the lobby and in the elevator, Bruce and his assistants, and he always has them carry his stuff for him.

It sounds like he has a girl with him. I turn off the lava lamp and pull back the rug. Bruce has put on some jazz.

After watching for a while I take a shower with a new Aveda product, complete body cleanser for the seventh chakra called Bliss. It's important to feel pure after being subjected to impure acts.

~

I hate Sundays.

Tongue looks pink with a yellowish cast. Basal
pulse rate, 70.

I feel weird on Sundays, like I'm lonely or something.

I practice the pencil drop with Sunshine—you have to be consistent with bird training. Then I figure I'll go to the library and look through the magazines and I'll bring my matte knife. I'll look through the *Times-Picayune* obituaries. It makes me feel peaceful to read about things that are resolved. And well-written. There's an elegance to death in the South. It's prettier back home. I think about saving a few of the most eloquent deaths, people with great names—they could be dignified or strange names, as long as they're not ordinary—and sending them to Wanda. She'd get a better idea about my true nature. She'd see that it's not just animals I love, but language, the art of writing. There's emotion in these words, these flat, polite and even overused expressions, a beauty to their simplicity. I even thought for a minute or two about working for a newspaper. But my analytical mind told me it would take all the pleasure out of it. There's no action. And think about how impossible those relatives would be. We won't be truly civilized until we have obituaries for pets. They could have songs written about them, too. Wanda and I could introduce a new genre of music. Wanda could compose music for little pet hymns and I could write the lyrics. I compose a postcard to Wanda in my mind.

Dear Wanda,

I would very much like to hear some of your compositions. I'm still hoping your music is sad. That if your music went with colors, they would be black and blue. Maybe some violet, too, like winter twilight over a dark lake or a fresh black eye.

Warmest regards, Pluto

Warmest regards, definitely. It's about time I show some feeling.

I squeeze two lemons for my morning liver cleanser and brush my teeth and tongue. I always brush my teeth before I feed the animals. I think it would be rude to hover over them with an unhygienic presence. Animals sense these things. I pick out an adorable goldfish, a vivid orange one with alert eyes, and scoop it up for Bacteria. I've grown to like the anonymity of these transient fish, here today, gone tomorrow. I don't ever let Bacteria see them before I put them in his aquarium—I keep a large piece of laminated board between their tanks, because Bacteria might start to get friendly with them.

Stripemaster and Stalin get to eat worms but this doesn't do anything for me. I think it's because worms don't have eyes.

Tuesday. Tongue pink with the faint coating like the first snowfall. Basal pulse, 72.

I'll walk dogs today and hope I run into Wanda.

I do. She's wearing the squirrel-colored shoes. No one who'd wear shoes like this could wear those big black bug shoes. Maybe Wanda has a sister.

"Wanda, are you an only child?" I ask, surprised at my directness.

"Why do you want to know?"

"I've heard that only children and firstborns are the achievers in the family. I'm an only child. I guess that's obvious."

Wanda gets this look, like she's trying to be stoic, like Marlon Brando in *Mutiny on the Bounty* when he's trying to look like he's not affected by the torture Captain Bligh's inflicting on the sailors but you can tell it's really getting to him.

"It seems strange that you should ask, that's all."

I don't say anything, but nod approvingly.

"I am sort of an only child."

I nod again, this time drawing my brows together, which is an expression that causes wrinkles but sometimes you have to show feeling. Facial expressions don't come naturally to me, but because I'm a compassionate person, I practice emotions in the bathroom mirror. I watch old movies with a hand mirror at my side so I can practice the best expressions. Animals have facial expressions. But they're too subtle for most people to read.

"They got me pets. Two ducks, a rabbit, a little pony

and an Irish setter. But it reminded me of her, you know, the red fur. And then, oh, never mind. I don't want to go into it."

"Of who?" I ask, letting my face become open and expressive and concerned, kind of like Billy Graham in old film footage.

"My sister. My little sister and, it's nothing."

I know for sure now that the blonde is not Wanda's sister, because if she's alive, she's a redhead, too. So who was it? Someone this deeply scarred and sensitive would be incapable of working in a topless bar. And if the sister is alive, she's probably just as sensitive, and by the sound of it, just as scarred. Maybe a cousin.

"Did you have cousins to play with?"

"Oh, yes," Wanda says. "Half a dozen, at least."

"Any of them in New York?"

"Why? Why do you want to know that? I hardly know anyone in New York. Not anymore."

"Let's pick out our dogs," I say lightheartedly. "We can talk on the way."

"If you don't mind, Pluto," Wanda says, "I'd like to walk alone."

"Of course," I say gallantly. I smile like I mean it. Why not? She's said my name! She's still in love with me.

She just feels overwhelmed. Let her walk alone. She'll feel lonely. She'll miss me. She'll be back.

I choose the young Irish setter, Charlotte, after Wanda leaves with a Dalmatian. As I walk Charlotte I decide that Wanda's music must have a melancholy, bruised quality, one that will be in harmony with my animal lyrics. Charlotte pulls hard on the leash like she wants to lead me somewhere. I let her lead. There's nothing wrong with her. She's been at the ASPCA for seven months, at least. It's her story that turns people off. Her owner died six or seven months after buying her. It was three days before they found him, and Charlotte with no food. She chose to starve, too decent to take chunks out of his leg, which she could have easily done, just jumped up to where he was hanging, they said the ceilings were low.

Charlotte is heading west. Maybe to where the guy used to live. Charlotte stops in front of a music store and barks.

"Do you want to go in?" I ask her. Charlotte sort of nods and gives me a pink-gummed smile, so I take her in. An old guy walks over to her and she licks his hand.

I hope he wasn't just handling money. Money is filthy. It could give her gum disease.

"Hey, Charlotte," he says. "Somebody walk you here today?"

"Where did you two meet?" I ask formally, but smiling like someone he can trust.

"Oh, it's a sad story. About her owner. He lived upstairs. Used to date a girl who works here."

He reaches behind a counter and pulls out a dog biscuit, not a good brand.

"I don't know why I still have these," he says.

They're probably stale. I feel like telling him to check the expiration date on the box.

"That's so thoughtful of you," I say cordially. "Who's the girl?"

"Wanda Swann. Maybe you know her. She's on her lunch hour right now walking dogs. She been walking dogs for the ASPCA ever since it happened."

I let the old man pet Charlotte.

"Nobody would take Charlotte. Wanda wouldn't take her. She wouldn't even take his piano. Lee, the guy, didn't have any living relatives in New York and it would have been easy enough to track them down with a name like his. Poissontête."

"What a weird name," I say, when I really mean it's a remarkable name. With a name like that we might have been friends. I even like the name Lee. It's not all that common. There was Lee Harvey Oswald and he was a rather provocative person.

"Weird guy. Ran some sort of sleazy club but he never talked about it. He got a lot of sheet music here, old-time racy stuff."

"Did he take Charlotte to the club with him?"

"Lee took Charlotte everywhere," says the old man.

Clubs are usually smoky. They're always smoky. Maybe he wasn't such a nice guy.

"Well, nice chatting with you, Mr. . . . "

"Rotstein. Stop by again."

I trot the reluctant Charlotte back to the ASPCA and make a mental addition to my ever-expanding list of cruelties humans inflict on animals.

1. Taking animals to bars or clubs that allow smoking. Includes establishments with cats or dogs actually living on the premises.

2. Leaving animals chained up outside in freezing weather while eating or shopping, etc.

3. Yelling around animals.

4. Using toxic chemicals for vanity like hair spray, or chemicals for work, such as spray mount, turpentine, or any art supplies with strong odors.

5. Using toxic household cleaning products such as ammonia on floors or other areas with which the animal has constant contact.

6. Mutilation of animals, such as tail or ear amputation for show-off effect or cutting off tips of cat's paws, a practice called declawing to "protect" furniture.

7. Babies. Subjecting an animal to a house with a newborn. The high-pitched and frequent screaming of the infant will terrorize the animal.

I can't seem to concentrate on copyediting when I get back to the office. I keep thinking about my mission. How I'll have to get Sunshine to go through my transom to rehearse. This is unlike me. I'm always focused. I enjoy my work. I've even, I can't believe I've done this, I've even chewed the tip of my pencil, a disgusting and unsanitary deed.

I hear this click, this cheap assertive click on the cheap office floors, and then I hear Camillia say, "Pluto. My, my."

Today she's in black. Tight black. And she's got on these elevator-type shoes, platforms, that give her an orthopedic whore look.

"You don't look like you're with us today," she says smugly.

I bite down harder on the pencil and the eraser snaps off in my mouth. It's her new editor-boss-slut-in-mourning look. They wear so much black in New York. Black, like depression or like death, like the dark busted-up tombs in the cemeteries, I'd crawl into them. The ceilings were low and thought-crushing, but it was a tomb, you weren't supposed to think in there, you were supposed to be sealed up in an artificial death, breathing in the old dirt and dust and mildew, breathing in millions of death spores. I remember the feeling, the exact feeling, it's like it's standing next to me, the loathsome sexy stillness and the kittens. A whole litter was entombed there, maybe the mother was coming back, maybe not, and I picked them all up and put them on my chest and felt their tiny hearts beating, small hearts, maybe as small as pinto beans, and their whiskers still soft and eyes still closed like they weren't officially alive yet. They were damp, and I thought about bringing them home, but Bill wouldn't like it, and I didn't have the dissection kit yet, which I admit is a selfish thing, just thinking about my own pleasure, even though it would advance my knowledge of the insides of things. I warmed them on my chest and let them hear my heart, bigger, stronger than all of them put together, the part of me that can love but can also hate and squish things until they pop. They wouldn't stay on me, though, and I kept gathering them up and they were squeaking and mewing and mewing in the spore-filled tomb, inhaling death with each tiny breath. I wanted them to like me, but they were already ruined and coldhearted and filled with a sense of motherless doom.

There were stone slabs in the tomb, the kittens could all be gathered and named—Horus, Nut, Osiris, Ra and Anubis—and put in one place. I could heave it down and take care of them all at the same time. There's something horrible in this, yes, I realized that, but naming them, I thought then, would ensure them a place in the afterlife and their eyes weren't even open yet. I mentioned that before. But I'm digressing.

Camillia raps her pencil on my desk to show off its smooth, unbitten surface, to show she's a calm but sexy executive and I see she's wearing a new color nail polish. A sort of punk slut raven black with some purple in it.

"Camillia," I say, smiling. The little pink eraser I bit off is stuck between my gum and molar. Probably making an unflattering lump in my cheek.

"You're such an unpredictable woman."

"Do you think so?" she says. She stops rapping the pencil.

"Your strength of character and individuality are always expressed by your careful choice of fashion."

"Careful? I look careful?"

"Well, mysterious, to be honest."

"You're such a lady-killer," Camillia says, rather genuinely too, and then clicks cheaply away.

From my desk I can see my reflection in the window. I look more handsome than usual. I can see that my bangs, which perfectly frame my dark, soulful eyes, need a trim. Saints probably had a countenance like mine, a gentle look with underlying conviction in the face of all obstacles and persecution. In the reflection I suddenly see Joey, the mouse-stomper, staring at me. He doesn't know I see him. He's probably thinking that I look handsome, that my destiny is chiseled in my cheekbones, which are fairly prominent, by the way. I accept his admiration, silently, internally. My time will come.

~

Wanda is pining away for me. I know this, because I've been timing my trips to the ASPCA so we'll just miss each other all week. This isn't easy for me. But she needs to understand that she can't be cold to me without repercussions. I take Charlotte out all week and have nice chats with Mr. Rotstein, always perfectly timed to be minutes after Wanda's left on her lunch hour. Mr. Rotstein is a very open man. The more I compliment him on his storytelling ability, how he should do voice-overs for fairy tales set to music, write them even, the more he tells me.

After dinner—organic steamed vegetables, it's a risk, I know, how can you be sure they're really organic—I go to the coffee shop across from Wanda's and have an orange juice. You should never combine acid foods like citrus with other foods, but it's an hour past dinner so I should be fine. I telephone her, get her machine and hang up. Then I compose a list of things to look for in Wanda's apartment in between staring at the impersonal glass doors of her building. At least they're clean, though the brass around them could use polishing. I can see the doorman, pushing the door open for the pig-faced woman. He's really careful not to touch the glass. He must be the one who cleans it. If somebody spilled a Coke or something on it, he'd run right out there and clean it. Probably have to leave the desk for a minute to get a cleaning cloth.

I wait outside the coffee shop on the lookout for a kid. A mercenary kid with vandalistic tendencies and a few ounces of idealism.

A kid with a Walkman bounces by, one of those

punks wearing his pants too big and too long so they look like they're about to fall off.

"Hey," I say, and loud, so he'll hear me over whatever. I act tough. "Come here," and I casually lean against the wall with my hands shoved in my pockets, I know it ruins the pockets, but it looks pretty cool. Like James Dean or that tragic dark-haired guy, Sal Mineo, in *Rebel Without a Cause*. Sometimes I worry that I'm too dramatic, that I'll come off as a phony.

The kid struts over. He pulls off his Walkman.

"You look like a smart kid, " I say.

"Yeah. So what?" says the kid.

"I need you to help me with a criminal act. In the name of love."

"What act? I ain't no criminal."

"I can see that. That's why I chose you."

"Yeah?" he says, falling for the flattery.

"In that building with the clean glass windows is the woman I love."

I point and he nods. "I have just written her a letter of proposal and I want to slip it under her door." I hold the folded letter up, which is sort of a love letter, my list of what to check when I get in her place. "I don't want the doorman to announce me."

"Just ask her, man."

"What?" I say.

"Why you asking her in a letter? You a wimp?" He looks me up and down. "Well, I guess it's your way, man."

I think it may be some sort of insult but I ignore it. I get a little tougher, though.

"Look, there's ten clams in it for you," I say, clams is a pretty cool word, one I figure he'll relate to.

"You're trippin'," says the kid. I ignore this insult, too.

"All you have to do, if you think you're fast enough, and your aim is good enough, is heave a beverage at that glass door."

"You gotta be kidding," says the kid. "Gimme the money."

"Not so fast. First, the grape drink, then the ten bucks."

I buy a can of grape drink in the coffee shop, ask for a big coffee container and pour it in. The kid crosses the street and throws the grape drink—perfect aim, too—sort of near the top of the door so it will run down, and then springs across the street where I'm watching from behind the tinted glass. I hand him the ten bucks and then he springs out of the shop.

The doorman, who is overweight, shakes his fists and

yells but he doesn't even run across the street after the kid. Probably too chicken. Then, just like I thought, the doorman disappears down the hall. I stride into the building like I belong there, casually looking at the mailboxes to see Wanda's apartment number, and head up to 5A.

Wanda is a beautiful, trusting and pure person. Not one of those neurotic, weird girls with an alarm and deadbolt. I knock first, of course, just to be sure, and then I easily unlock her door with a few quick repetitions with a credit card, Bill's, who showed me how to do this in the first place. My heart is fluttering like birds being shot at, and I have to remind myself that I'm in control, that I'm the hunter, not the hunted, and there's no rational reason to be nervous. Wanda isn't home.

Once unlocked the door opens, slowly, like a gentle invitation. I close it quietly behind me and inhale. It smells like Wanda. And animals. There's a distinctive wild animal odor, a savage vapor layered under a clean Ivory soap scent. And everything is white and natural and virginal. She even leaves slippers by the door, which means she changes out of her shoes when she gets home. The first thing I do is put on my surgical gloves, I wouldn't want to leave fingerprints, what if Wanda dies or something, they'd think I did it, and check out the kitchen. Just like I thought. Ivory dishwashing detergent, the old-fashioned white kind, not the new clear stuff. The stove is spotless, though there's a tea stain or something brownish in the sink, maybe from years of dropping a tea bag there, but, heck, nobody's perfect. There's a mug from her trip to Las Vegas. I don't understand why someone as sweet as Wanda would want to go to Las Vegas. Who'd she go with, that Lee guy? She's got thirteen plates, matching, and matching smaller ones and bowls, too, but only eleven each of those, in the cupboard, white with a classic navy band around them and no chips, I check all of them. She cleans the undersides of plates, too, that's important. This means we're compatible. Except I can't figure out why anyone in their right mind would need thirteen plates. I check her pet bowls, that's always telling, and see the missing bowls. I like that she shares her china with her animals, it's like she's invited them to dinner. She has several kinds of tea, herbal tea and Twinings, an excellent brand, and in the refrigerator, mineral water but no mucous-producing dairy products. But there's ketchup, which seems strange. Unless it's that redheads are attracted to tomatoes or red foods or something like that. A subconscious thing. She doesn't have a water filter, though. Does she boil all her water? Does she give her pets mineral water or boil their water? I'm sure she must know there are over two thousand chemicals in New York City water, and parasites.

There's a tiny living room, just an alcove really, that looks like her music studio. She's got instruments all over—an electric guitar, two acoustic guitars, one in wood and one in steel with no finger smudges on it, a big Casio keyboard, lots of electronic-looking black boxes and a microphone. I guess Wanda sings here, inspired by the stirrings of her animals and her private thoughts. Who am I to guess what those might be, but I suspect they're romantic and memorable times we've spent together.

It's all very neat except for a mess of black cords criss-crossed all over the floor like squid-ink spaghetti or worms. At least the heaps of music paper are in folders in neat stacks and the shelves of cassettes are organized by dates, though I was hoping they would be arranged alphabetically by title, maybe titles like "Chinatown with Pluto," or "I Saw Pluto at the ASPCA Today," or "Watching Pluto's Pets."

Now the bedroom. Before I check the photo by the bed I pick up the comforter and look at her sheets, which are a little wrinkled and pulled up unevenly at the top. White. I'm so relieved. I couldn't handle it if they had some ugly pattern on them, like a bogus Pompeii pattern or rainbows or, God forbid, roses. Well, maybe dolphins would be okay. Wamsutta, 100 percent cotton. Not tucked in at the corners, but not a total mess either. The bottom sheet is the same brand as the top, which shows a sense of organization and consistency in aesthetics. God, I hate it when sheets don't match. And there's cat fur. You'd think a Virgo would hate cat fur on sheets, but I think it lends a warm, natural quality to something otherwise pristine.

I look on her dresser, an old dark mahogany one, polished like fancy-dress shoes, with a runner made of a deep ivory lace that looks like it might be from Europe. The mirror is on a hinge and she's dangled, rather recklessly in that way feminine women do, a few pearl-colored necklaces over the corners. There are two gaudy gold chains that don't fit in. They spell out names. One says LEE and the other one says LOULOU. This is disturbing. Could LouLou be her middle name? I open the top drawer—I have a strong feeling I'll find a passport in there, and under a soapy-scented heap of stockings and sensuous mounds of peach-and-ivory-colored silk things—I spread them all out on the bed just to check out her lingerie taste—is her passport, the key to really important things. Birth date and legal name.

Wanda Marie Sirenidae Ennis Swann.

March 2, 1967.

She's a sheep, too. That means we can get along together as a team. I knew all along she was a Pisces, but she must have Virgo in her chart somewhere to be this neat, though not too much Virgo, look at this underwear drawer. And there's that stain in the sink. It's a relief to know her real name is Wanda, and not Pam, and that she has five names. She must be Catholic, they get to choose extra names at confirmation.

I take off the gloves so I can have physical contact with Wanda's things and I almost lose track of time. Some of this stuff is really beautiful, but simple, classic. I'd even look good in some of it. I lie facedown on her silky peachy things, I know it's something a pervert would do, but I'm in love, and I feel more intimate with her this way, then I put it all away in the same careless heaps as I found them. There's some other scent besides the soap and cleanness. Like violets.

It's kind of an old-fashioned perfume but with a flooziness about it. One minute it smells violently purple like it's laughing, and then it disappears. It's unpredictable and sweet and a little depressing, like a Pisces. Napoleon's wife Josephine—I wonder if she was a Pisces, I can't believe I don't know that—wore violet perfume. Napoleon even planted violets on her grave. I'd plant violets on Wanda's grave. I remember reading that when Napoleon was exiled in 1814, I think it was 1814, he picked some of the violets and kept them in a locket or something for the rest of his life. It's romantic, but if Wanda died, I'd need something more tangible. Maybe I'd take a tooth or a bone fragment.

I don't know how she can stand not having anything up on the bedroom walls, and I mean nothing. Doesn't she feel lonely? Maybe she likes feeling lonely. I guess having pets is enough. The marmosets are in a substantial cage near the window. The rabbit is sleeping in a helpless lump. The cats are piled up near the rabbit but the lemur, I don't see anywhere. Then I get a good look at the guy by the bed. He's in a cheap brass frame, and he's almost making out with a big Irish setter. I recognize the dog. It's Charlotte. That means the guy is Lee Poissontête. Charlotte's got her paws on his chest—the dog had the good sense to try to cover up his hideous T-shirt—but I can still make it out. It says MEGADETH. He's smiling but it doesn't work. Narrow and economical, his mean little mouth only manages mock happiness. And the worst part, he's wearing a hat, a baseball hat, that says BUDWEISER. His hair's probably thinning on top, or he's bald and I just can't see Wanda with a bald guy. The worst part of him is his mouth. The top lip is too thin and the bottom lip is blubbery, like a grouper's. No, the worst part is his teeth. One is darkened, the color of feathers on a pigeon, one is capped, definitely, a totally different color from his natural enamel, and there's a chipped tooth. Why is he bothering with the phony smile with teeth like this? Is he just thrilled to get his picture taken with Charlotte or is he in love? Who took this picture? That's what I hate about photos. You can't tell who took them. The documentation is so shabby. I mean, he's making this expression for a particular person and if it's Wanda who evoked it, I'm devastated.

This is crazy. How can you know who takes a picture, it's just a snapshot. So what if it's Lee Poissontête. I'm getting too worked up. It's Wanda, I can't picture her with anyone but me, how could she even look at another man, how could she ever have looked at another man?

I should take his picture out of the frame and put one of me in there, I mean, the guy was a loser. What's he standing in front of anyway, I wonder, a tacky obscene poster of a girl, I can only see part of it but she's got a whip and tall black boots in some synthetic material.

Yeah, I should get a picture of me with Charlotte, I'd get it taken from the most flattering angle. But who would take it? It's a nice little fantasy, anyway.

I check out the bathroom. Very clean. Tub clean too, no ring. No mold on the edges of the shower curtain, either. And she turns the faucets off all the way, I hate it when people don't turn them off all the way and they drip.

Little shells are heaped decoratively on the floor and around the shower ledge and they look pretty, sort of remind me of my skull collection. Shells are the external bones of sea creatures, after all. Nothing on the walls in here, either, not even a postcard. She would have put my postcards up if I'd actually written them. Taped them up, or maybe put them in frames.

There's a shelf with a basket with hair stuff in it, a mock tortoiseshell comb and a brush, the kind they make in France, a good one. Some hairs are left in it but I guess that's inevitable when you have long hair. The horrifying thing is that some of them are blonde and I sure didn't use it. I'd never share a comb or brush with a human, or a towel for that matter, unless it was my wife and it was an emergency.

I feel uneasy about this and back out of the bathroom

to leave but I can feel something or someone staring at me. I look up and I'm startled to see the lemur, a ring-tailed lemur, on top of the shower curtain rod, and it's laughing at me.

~

I get home and take off my shoes. I can't believe I've been forgetting to do this lately. I've been tracking God knows what from the streets all over my apartment floor and Le Sang could pick up an infection or a disease from this careless behavior. I put a voluptuous goldfish into Bacteria's tank. He sucks it into his mouth but gulping it down he severs the head, which floats unblinkingly and meaningfully to the surface and then slowly sinks.

I feel sort of hungry then, ravenous, in fact, so I put tofu and kale in the pot to steam and add a little ginger, but not so much it will be overwhelming. I like subtle, tasteful things.

When I sit down to eat—I use a placemat, I'm not a typical bachelor that way, I guess—Sunshine flies over to my plate and drops the aluminum-foil-covered pencil into it. I'm going to have to start her with the vials soon.

"Good girl," I say. "But not yet."

I've been drinking a lot of vodka lately. It's healthier than beer, it's so clear and biting, it sort of clears my mind. Alcohol is my only weakness and everyone needs a vice in order not to be a mundane human. It's one of the only good differences between animals and humans. Humans can handle alcohol. We need it to cope. I feel creative when I drink. I've been making cranberry and vodka drinks. Real cranberry juice, not that cocktail stuff with artificial sweetener. After my fifth one—five must be my lucky number, Wanda's apartment number—I resolve to do a little more transom training with Sunshine for "Operation Sunshine." We'll start with the cats that live a tortured, tumultuous existence with the disco Budweiser couple.

The whole week I feel calm. Sunshine rehearses every day with me, through the transom of my apartment, and I regularly move the water bowl around so she gets used to dropping the vial in different places. I plug up the vials with a cotton ball through which liquids can penetrate.

After our last rehearsal, Sunshine and I take a shower using Chakra VII Bliss Complete Body Cleanser to put us in an elevated state of mind and at 9:30 A.M. when the disco couple leaves for work, late as usual, which they argue about every day, because one of them always forgets to set the alarm, I stand quivering in the hallway with Sunshine on my arm. The air reeks near the Budweiser couple's door. Hair spray. A perfume that smells a lot like bug spray on plastic flowers, and cigarettes. When I go to push open the transom I can smell kitty litter, too. How often do they change it? The transom is locked. No problem. I still have Bill's credit card and if that doesn't work, a piece of wire. I get my chair and put some paper towels over it so I can stand on it to reach the transom and easily open it with a wire. I really want to watch, at least this first time, but it's too risky to leave the chair in the hall.

I hand the vial to Sunshine and point to the transom. I kiss her on the head and her black wings open and she ascends, perching lightly on the transom ledge and looking back at me before her descent. I imagine her circling around the apartment and casting foreboding shadows over the sleeping cats and swooping down, dropping the vial into a dingy water bowl, so dingy it probably has fungus growing in it.

The cats, however, are not sleeping. I hear them hissing, screaming, probably lunging at Sunshine and trying to scratch out her eyes. Not that I blame them. That's their job. They don't know I'm doing them a favor. That doesn't make me any less of a wreck, however, and by the time Sunshine wings out, I realize I've been so tense I've been holding my breath. I jump up and close the transom and then reward Sunshine with an M&M. I'm late for work, of course, but sometimes you have to write your own rules.

He comes home first. He's carrying a case of Budweiser, a pizza and a bag from Dunkin' Donuts. No kitty litter, which they sorely needed. I hear him cursing, which seems like a weird reaction to me. In a few minutes, she comes home.

"How could you do this," he's screaming.

"Do what!" she yells.

Then I guess he holds one of them up or points to them because she goes out of control. I wish they'd keep it down, but I have no one to blame but me for all the racket.

I take a walk through the building taking mental notes of my next target. Nancy Stanlostovich, 2B. Leaves her German shepherd chained up in front of her health club in bitter weather for entire workouts taking up to two hours, but to look at her, you'd never know she went to a health club. She also makes the dog carry milk cartons and, worse, newspapers without giving any thought to his ingesting dubious quantities of newsprint ink.

~

By the following week Sunshine and I have done our work in four apartments. There's a bulletin on the door in the lobby warning people to keep their pets under lock and key, and the super, who doesn't have a pet and is the kind of guy dogs instinctively want to bite, is suspected of breaking into all the apartments since he has the keys, after all, and knows everyone's schedules.

Somehow, my work, I mean our work—Sunshine should get some of the credit—called the Chelsea Animal Slayings, gets in the paper. The *New York Post*, of course, with a big photo of two cats who've finally found peace, and it's all anyone at the ASPCA can talk about. It gives me a tingling feeling to hear people talk about it, and an even stronger feeling in my gut when I see something in print, though I worry it's going to give me a big ego. I start a scrapbook. By the time I get to some of the lower floors of my building I'm sure the *New York Times* will be writing about us. It's best, I'm sure, if I say as little as possible since it is my building but I do say, to Wanda, "Has anyone ever thought about the common denominator between all the pet owners? Like maybe they were all abusive in some way?"

Wanda's eyes widen so they look entirely too blue. I try to imagine her as a Siamese cat. "Do you think so?" she says.

"Well," I say. "I do live in the building. Don't you think it's a little odd that they didn't go after my pets?"

"How do you know they won't?" she says.

"I don't," I say, and I mean it.

While she's in this heightened, vulnerable state I invite her for a drink at my apartment Saturday evening, and tell her Mom's birthday is coming up in a few days, she's an Aquarius and her health is worse, by the way, and that I've written her a poem, lyrics, actually, that I'd like to set to music. Wanda offers to compose something on her keyboard. "I'll pick you up," I say.

"I've got work Saturday evening," she says. "Why don't I stop by on my way, at like five-thirty?"

The days until Saturday are filled with a robust sense of anticipation, pet grooming and cleaning. I vacuum Bacteria's tank, clean the windows with vinegar and newspapers and shake the bear rug. As I'm cleaning the glass on the lava lamp, it's funny how cleaning can clear your mind, I realize I need to buy another drinking glass. I put the vodka in the freezer. I want everything to be perfect. And flowers. I need flowers. She'll know I'm a sensitive, kind person if I have flowers—in light of what I have to tell her. Not violets, though. I need flowers that will express my particular brand of sensitivity, something more masculine. I could get cobra lilies. Or maybe a plant, like a Venus flytrap.

I think I'll wear my smoking jacket.

The timing couldn't be better. As Wanda comes in— she takes her shoes off—the catless disco Bud couple is leaving. The woman looks particularly disheveled and her eye makeup is runny and the guy looks like hell, like he's been up all night watching colorized films and washing down unchewed gulps of Velveeta and Spam and donuts with Budweiser.

"Wanda," I say, "just look at them. Take a good look."

Wanda looks through the peephole.

"Heavens," she says.

"See what I mean?" I say. They're fumbling with the keys, it's taking them forever, they're both so clumsy.

"Those people look so unhappy, like someone's just died or something."

"Aren't they awful? Did you see the nails on her? Would you want them looking after your pets?"

Wanda turns around and looks at me.

"You don't think they did it, do you?"

"Did what?" I say, just to see how she'll express this.

"The Animal Slayings?" she says.

Typical. Typical. Wanda automatically goes for the *Post* headline instead of seeing the compassion behind my actions. The media is too influential. I'll have to write them a letter, clear things up. It's not her fault, I guess. She's never heard my side. And the *Post* is certainly not known for balanced reportage. I mean, the coverage is exciting but misses the point.

"Of course I don't think they saved any animals," I say.

"Saved?" says Wanda.

"I don't mean saved as in saving their lives, I wasn't articulate."

"That's a relief," says Wanda. She puts down two big black bags, one must be the keyboard and the other is zipped most of the way so it's hard to see what's in there.

Then she pulls off her gloves, gracefully, like Grace Kelly, and places them on the partially zipped bag.

"Please, sit down," I say and pull out my chair the way I've seen gentlemen do in movies. I can sit on the edge of the table. Or stand. That would be impressive. I'll look more powerful if I tower over her, my Venus flytrap between us on the table so I'll appear complex. Sensitive and life-loving, but masterful and commanding, like Napoleon, but taller of course. "May I get you a drink?" I smile at her, knowing I'm irresistible.

"Water would be fine," Wanda says.

I go to the freezer and pour two vodkas and I can see Wanda about to protest, so I say, "Don't worry, I can afford it. Cranberry juice?"

She nods. The glasses are chilled, our drinks are pink like a carnival, like rosy-pink carnival animals we've won together. The color looks good with my smoking jacket.

Wanda clinks her glass against mine, timidly, and a piece of red hair, brilliant like the yarn hair on Judy Baker's doll, falls recklessly over her forehead and whole-some eyebrows. They're so furry, like a fennec fox, I want to pet them, but I don't want her to think I'm kinky, into facial hair or something. If I had to choose between pet-ting her eyebrows or nibbling on that fleshy web between her thumb and index finger, I'd take the web. Not hard, though, just love bites. I wonder if there are more nerve endings in the weasel's webs or Wanda's.

She takes a dainty sip.

"Don't you like it?" I ask her and Wanda says yes she does, it's just that she's got to work later.

I'm about to take the direct approach and ask where, when Le Sang weasels into the room and heads for her partially unzipped bag.

"I hope you don't have any rubber in there?"

Wanda looks puzzled. Then she blushes.

"Like a Swatch," I say, explaining Le Sang's fondness for rubber. Gracious host that I am, I reach for her bag to get it away from Le Sang, but Wanda darts her hand past mine like a piranha going after prey and tugs the bag toward her.

Frankly, I'm stunned. She has an aggressive competitive streak. I guess I'm supposed to think that's exciting. Unless she doesn't want me to know what's in there.

"You should put it on the counter," I tell her and explain that vets are always taking rubber obstructions out of ferret stomachs and intestines, troll hands, rubber bands, parts of sink stoppers, you name it.

I stand so the window's behind me. The last shreds of

light will give me an unearthly glow, kind of a halo, and I read her the lyrics, starting out kind of soft, but crisp as an ironed shirt, and then build to a dramatic crescendo, like Vincent Price, only not so melodramatic:

Bird of omen, saving grace

Winging toward her goal with haste

Sweeping clean the path of sorrow

For evanescent light tomorrow

Erasing thieving karmic debt *(Here I remind Wanda that Mom thinks Sunshine is a reincarnation of Barabbas, the thief released instead of Christ)*

With grieving thoughts for every pet

Black wings, black eyes

Black feet, sweet cries

Sunshine in her mercy flight

Feathers darkness with slumbers of light.

Wanda doesn't say anything for a minute—that's characteristic of sensitivity, and she's got that stunned, impressed look.

"You know," I tell her, lowering my eyes to convey modesty, "I studied late-nineteenth-century poetry at Tulane."

Wanda says she can tell so I ask her if she thinks it's too derivative and explain that I've taken liberties with the style, improved it, in fact.

I can tell she's already imagining the music, she seems anxious to start—she's tapping her fingers on the kitchen table, if it were anyone else, the sound would make me nuts, and I suggest she put the keyboard on the kitchen table. I'm not worried about her scratching it up. She has paper in the case, composition paper, but she studies my lyrics before she does anything.

I hadn't expected her to hum while she read them. I feel like pressing my fingers on her lips and throat, which I imagine would pulse gently, like kittens purring, and she purrs for a while longer and I drink another vodka cranberry.

Then Wanda sings. She sounds kind of like a bird. Not chirpy, like a sparrow, nasal like a budgie or parrot or deeply resonant like a raven's quork. It's something more exotic or maybe even undiscovered, like a delicate red and ivory bird with a silvery trilling with cooing undertones.

BIRD OF OMEN

Bird of O - men, s - a - ving gra - ce,

wing - ing toward her goal with haste

Sweep - ing clean the path___ of sor - row

For ev - an - es - cent light to - mor - row

E - ras - ing thiev - ing kar ___ mic debt with

Griev - ing thoughts for ev - ery pet

Bl - a___ck wings Bl - a___ ck eyes

Bl - a___ ck feet Sw - e___ et cries

Sun ___ shine in her mer ___ cy fli - ght,

Feath - ers the dark - ness with a slum - ber of

light

I knew my lyrics were good but I'm genuinely surprised they sound this good, the kind of lyrics that can
move someone. She's playing with some sort of organ
effect on her keyboard that makes me think of cathedrals
and heaps of skulls and tall stained-glass windows with
blackbirds soaring like thunderclouds.

I almost feel, for a minute, that I must have been meant
to be a musician, or destined to meet a musician. I'm sure
it's no accident I make spin art on my record player.

As Wanda's fingers move on the keys I think about
her running her hands through my hair, even messing up
my bangs. I bet she'd love to do that. Girls are into hair.
Messing it up, brushing it, cutting it, anything. It makes
them feel powerful and maternal. Maybe even sexy. Maybe
I ought to ask her over to give me a haircut, that would be
intimate. But somehow, I don't think a Pisces could cut
bangs straight. A Pisces would try to do something orig-
inal, and I'm a classical guy when it comes to hair.

I have a drawer in the kitchen where I keep supplies.
Not just veterinary stuff, but rubber bands, paper clips
and pens. Not loose, of course, they're in boxes, preferably
the ones they came in, otherwise I mark them—so I go to
the pen box and take out my fountain pen which is next
to the syringes.

"Please, here," I say. "Here's a pen."

She makes fast but perfect notes and purple ink flows out like a gently opened vein.

She doesn't finish her drink and I think about drinking it after she leaves except I can't be sure which side she drank out of, she doesn't have on lipstick. She never wears lipstick. I think that should make me want to kiss her, seeing her lips naked like this and I do want to, except when I think about germs. Even people you love can have germs, and it probably takes a while to get used to someone else's bacteria and pH level. I wonder if my breath is bad right now, if I do kiss her. On the cheek, maybe.

Wanda settles back into the chair and looks at the music she's written and says she'll have to finish it at home on her four-track where she can add in the guitar, too. She picks up the keyboard—I unplug it—and gently eases it into the case, and while she's doing this I see Sunshine with this crazed beady look she gets when she sees something shiny. A gold chain—I'm assuming it's real gold—spills out of Wanda's shirt. The words on it say LouLou. Wanda sees me staring at it, and then sees Sunshine staring at it and she looks nervous, like she got caught shoplifting or something. Maybe LouLou is her cousin, I'm thinking, the blonde one. That would explain everything.

Without me even having to ask Wanda says, "It was a gift. A stage name." And she tucks it back in her shirt. She's blushing now, and her pearl-colored skin—she's not the kind of redhead with freckles, but I'd love them if she had them—flushes until she's a familiar shade of pink, the color of the pink dog.

I imagine this must be some kind of joke gift, giving a classical composer the kind of name that belongs to a showgirl with big hair and a French poodle. I tell Wanda this and she laughs, putting her hand up to her delicate throat. She throws her head back like a little horse, kind of convulsively, actually, but I guess I'm just funnier than I realize. A woman can make you see how funny you are, and then she kisses me—hard—on the cheek. When she leaves I go to the bathroom mirror to see if there's a mark, or some kind of glow—I felt so sure there would be some sort of difference. I almost wish she'd kissed me on the lips. I'm distracted from this revelation by a knock on the door. Wanda's come back. She's going to embrace me. I can handle it. I pat down my bangs and open the door without checking first and boy, is that a mistake. It's the Budweiser couple. They just stand there.

"Yes?" I say politely. "How may I help you?"

"Hi. Darlene and Roy from across the hall," he says.

"The police aren't doing anything," she says.

"Excuse me?" I say. "

"About what's going on," he says.

"To all the animals," she says. She blows her nose on a wet, ratty blue tissue with lipstick marks and eye makeup on it. "We loved our cats."

She doesn't love animals. She loves drama. This is probably the most exciting thing that's ever happened to her. I almost wish I hadn't given her this sense of having been singled out, a sense of importance.

"Please, come in," I say. "Let me get you some tissues."

"Do you have pets?" he asks.

"Yes, I do." I offer her a box of white tissue.

"Then maybe you can help us," he says. "We want to post a watchperson at the door, twenty-four hours. Even though it's too late for us. And some of the others."

She squeezes his pudgy, hairy hand. "We'll get kittens, Roy. Persian kittens or Siamese."

I hate killing expensive animals.

"Why not get cats or kittens from the ASPCA or the North Shore Animal League," I suggest, but these types never want rejected animals.

"Thanks," she says, "but we don't want an animal that's been traumatized."

"Yes, I know," I say, sounding sincere, because I do mean it, after all. "Trauma is terrible for animals." I wonder for a moment if Operation Sunshine is the wrong approach to the problem. This couple thinks you just replace pets like car parts. Or mayonnaise. If it goes bad, you get a new jar.

Darlene starts to pick a hangnail. "Why us? They didn't get Mrs. Hedges' dog."

"Isn't she the one with the miniature collie?"

"Yes, why our pets, and not hers?"

It hasn't occurred to them that Mrs. Hedges treats her dog properly. She doesn't smoke or use typical female chemical products. She gives her dog a little coat during the winter and cleans his paws off with a soft rag before she admits him into her apartment. She never leaves him chained up outside and once I saw her at a cafe with a gentleman and she paid just as much attention to her dog as the man.

"Or why not yours?" says Darlene.

"I don't have the kind of mind that can figure out that kind of thing," I say and smile like someone nice but a little feebleminded. "But I'd be happy to pitch in."

"The weirdest thing, and it wasn't in the papers, was everyone whose pet was killed found a test tube in their pet's dish."

"How horrible," I say, looking shocked. "I hope the deaths were painless."

Darlene looks at Roy like I've said something meaningful, something that she hadn't considered. She sobs.

"Yes, yes, I'm sure they didn't feel a thing," Roy says.

"They probably just fell asleep," I offer brightly.

"Thank you. We'll stay in touch," Roy says, and grasps my hand roughly, firmly, as if to say, "Men understand these things. Aren't women emotional."

Camillia knows about Wanda. I don't know how, but she does. I overheard her telling the art director to make the next cover of the *Pancreas Journal* violet. She used just that word. Not purple. Not lavender. Not eggplant. But violet. Maybe I'm getting paranoid. Maybe it's that she's seen what I've been writing in violet ink, Wanda Wanda Wanda, at least thirty-seven times on my yellow legal pad. Or the violet candies I keep in my top drawer. I know they cause cavities but they remind me of Wanda, of lying on her peachy violet-scented things on her bed. I'm sure Camillia is jealous. I don't blame her, in a way, I'm the only handsome, intelligent and sensitive guy around.

Before I leave for lunch—I have to get out of here, I have a splitting headache, there's a chemical smell in here—I casually drop corrected galleys on Camillia's desk.

"Thank you, Pluto," she says without looking up. Not thanks, but, "Thank you Pluto," which gives me the feeling that something's wrong.

"Can I get you something?" I say in my most charming way and Camillia looks up. She's wearing violet lipstick, fuchsia actually, but it's about as close to violet as you get, and violet nail polish. She probably did her nails in the office, that's why I have a headache. Why does she want to upset me like this? Does she want me to quit?

"I'd love some aspirin," she says. "No, make it Advil, my head is pounding." I nod and smile, but sympathetically.

I have this fantasy suddenly where I say, "Did you say pounding?" and I pick up a hammer, a good one with a heavy wooden handle, and give her skull a few good pounds and she puts her hands up to her head and her violet nails clash with the blood. This gives me an idea for a spin-art piece mixing violets and reds. And I could glue Advils all over it.

"Thanks, Pluto," Camillia says and, overcome with gratitude, she reaches out with her violet hands and messes up my bangs. I think about cutting off the tips of her fingers in the paper cutter.

"Gosh," I say, smiling as if I enjoyed it.

~

Tacked to the corkboard at the ASPCA is a padded envelope for me. It's from Wanda. It's the composition paper with the lyrics written above the notes and two cassettes, one tied in violet ribbon, really nice ribbon, not the flimsy kind that would tear if you tied somebody up with it. Mom will get one for her birthday. And I'll have to buy a tape player so I can listen to it, when I wake up, before I go to sleep, while I'm in the shower, eating dinner, pretty much during all my free time.

Wanda's birthday is coming up soon. I'll spin her a painting. I'll sign in my neatest handwriting in violet ink, or better yet, blood.

I spin twenty-seven paintings and choose my favorite. I add a "W" with four of Sunshine's feathers and staple them on. I'd like to prove my love but I feel too queasy to jab my finger. I sign it in violet ink,

Love, Pluto

I think about the word *love*. You don't need to bleed for someone to prove you love them. It's more about looking out for them. Eyes are what I need. I'll pick up some glass animal eyes at that taxidermy place on West 36th Street. I'll glue them on all around the "W."

~

I hope Wanda's not the type of person who takes a holiday from responsibility on her birthday. If she shows up at the ASPCA I can give her my art piece. I've gotten very attached to it. It's the best thing I've ever made. I think it's a masterpiece.

I pretend to be reading my newspaper, the *Weekly World News*. When she comes in I act surprised.

Wanda may think it's strange that I know it's her birthday.

"I never properly thanked you for writing that heart-breakingly beautiful music. It was the perfect complement to my lyrics," I say. I hand her the painting, which I've wrapped with the "pets" section of the *New York Times*.

"Thank you," says Wanda. "You didn't have to."

Her eyes widen when she sees it. She loves it. She seems overwhelmed by emotion.

"I've never seen anything like it," she says.

Frankly, I was hoping she'd be a little more exuberant and say something like, "Pluto, darling, it's a masterpiece."

But all she adds is, "Thank you." Then she looks at me strangely. "Did you know today is my birthday?"

"No. You're kidding."

I lift her delicate hand to my mouth and kiss the smooth hollow between her knuckles. I could almost nibble on the little web.

"Happy birthday," I say. "May you have many many more."

~

I have to wait until April for the Children's Zoo in the Bronx Zoo to open. Then I take the 2 train to Tremont Avenue to check it out. At a lot of the subway stops I see those new posters from the ASPCA.

There is no safe sex for animals.

This is a very cool idea to get people to neuter their animals. But the people who most need to neuter them probably can't read. Humans ought to exercise a little restraint when it comes to breeding. They should put signs up using symbols. It seems like there's a baby getting in at nearly every subway stop. What kind of mother takes a baby on the subway? I'm sure it will damage their eardrums. Why do they breed if they can't afford to take cabs? Not that I'd pick up a woman with a baby if I were a cab driver.

I pay $1.50 to get into the Children's Zoo. Kids under two years old get in free. I don't get that. They should charge extra for letting kids in. It's hard to maneuver past all the strollers of blubbery, squinty-eyed, toothless little blobs with fat, uncoordinated hands. And the mothers are walking so slowly. But as much as I hate strollers, the older kids are worse because they're so jumpy and gummy and loud. Most of the animals in the Children's Zoo are safely inaccessible. But the fences are low, low enough to throw things over or climb in and be disturbed with screaming, yelling and other things kids do. I see a kid throw a quarter at a sleeping fennec fox. Nobody gave me money to throw away at that age. Why the hell should the fox wake up to entertain the little brat? To him, and all the other brats, the animals are just anonymous entertainment, miserably on display. They don't even post their names. The animals are like parts, replaceable parts. If an otter dies, chokes on a Pez dispenser or something, they'll just get another one.

Research, that's a cool, exciting, functional sort of sacrifice. I get goose bumps just thinking about some of the material I get to edit at work. But entertainment? Isn't television enough?

The petting zoo is worse. Children jab their fingers through a fence and feed sheep and goats food from a dispenser machine, but what's to prevent them from giving the animal gum or poison, for that matter, or keep them from stabbing sharp instruments into the animals' mouths or eyes? Didn't anybody think of that? Do they think children are sweet-natured and innocent? Animals are the first thing a kid with a mean streak starts to torture. If I were that type of kid I'd start with the baby lamb, the sweet bleating little white lamb.

I knew there was going to be something really upsetting here and just before I leave I see it. A girl with unwashed hair and wearing brown-polyester blend pants, a little too tight, of course, will take your kid's portrait with an animal. A sedated-looking guinea pig is lying on a kid's lap like a wet mitten, sparing, for a moment, an exhausted rabbit collapsed in a small carrying case and a nervous hen pacing in a tiny cage.

This is like purgatory for them. Or hell. Locked up in a little container like Chinese takeout and only taken out to be squeezed and squished and held by awkward, sticky, dirty children hands.

It almost makes you think you're going nuts or something when you see all these parents standing around and laughing like it's perfectly normal and acceptable to see animals suffer like this. Sometimes I feel like I'm the last compassionate person on earth.

Still, it does seem like a great opportunity to have my picture taken so Wanda can replace Lee's with mine. After the kid leaves I ask the girl in brown to take my picture, without an animal, of course. I decide to take the straight-on approach; direct and sincere, like someone you can trust. The girl looks through the camera and adjusts its height.

"Smile," she says. I like that idea. The idea of smiling for Wanda. I ask to borrow a mirror to check my expression because sometimes it's hard to tell if you're doing it right.

On my way out, I see how easily I'd be able to get into the zoo at night. There's a patch of fence right near the wall without barbed wire. I could scale it and reach over to the wall adjacent to it and jump down to the soft soil. Or I could hide out in a wooded area, like near the trumpeter swans, until everyone leaves.

~

Camillia has on a tight brown pantsuit on Monday. I wonder if she knows I went to the zoo.

At lunch I plan to run into Wanda at the ASPCA. I've avoided her most of the winter and concentrated on finishing my work in the apartment building. The super quit and nobody wants the job.

~

I buy a camouflage jumpsuit at a dumpy-looking store on Canal Street, one with polyester, but I can't find 100 percent cotton and I'll only be wearing it for a few hours if I go over the fence. I can't see doing it any other way because polyester is so offensive. It makes you sweat and it feels like you're wearing a chemical. I'm sure your body absorbs polyester, and as I'm thinking this I realize I'm being selfish, thinking about my own comfort. The smart thing to do is hide out in the dark so I can glom the layout—I heard that expression in a movie once—and I can always wear a long-sleeved T-shirt under the jumpsuit.

～

Right before closing time I amble over to my hiding place not far from the Children's Zoo. There's an intoxicating animal fragrance that I catch in whiffs now and then, and I feel like a predator, the kind who chooses his prey by scent. I settle down to wait for the workers to leave. Not only do I feel like a predator, I feel like a soldier. I pull out my Deco stainless-steel flask filled with healthy cranberry juice and a little vodka. The initials on the flask aren't mine—I've thought of everything—just in case I drop it or something. And I'm wearing rubber gloves.

Listening to the Walkman—I broke down and got one—while I wait is a risk. I should be listening for patrol activity but this is a matter of heart. I blend into the landscape and listen to *Bird of Omen* and take another swig from my flask. It's as though my sensitivity is heightened, even through the gloves the silver flask feels cool—a gentleman's flask has a temperature, I'm thinking, a disposition.

A predator is not cruel or sadistic. People have a hard time with that idea. It's fine to eat a hamburger but God forbid an owl should swoop down and snare a little rodent. People think rodents are cute if an owl is eating them but they're not if they're running around in the house or stuck in a glue trap. An owl, or any predator, doesn't think about the suffering it causes. In that sense, I'm superior to animal killers. My method is painless and I have the qualities—rare in most people—of pity and mercy.

Also rare is an analytical mind. I have also chosen this night carefully. The moon is full, so I won't need to use a flashlight, and better yet, it's in Virgo. It's a methodical, helpful, intelligent kind of atmosphere. I would never do this, say, if there was going to be a lunar eclipse. Presidents who ignore astrology puke at important dinner functions in Japan during lunar eclipses.

Hours pass and I hear a lot of employees leave but I don't want to be hasty. The sky is pulsing with a faint light and the trees stand against it like a garden of skeletons. When I'm 99.9 percent sure everyone's gone I make my way, silently, toward the Children's Zoo. My eyes are used to the dark and this is better than being in my bedroom with all my pictures. Animals' eyes glitter like stars. White teeth flash in the moonlight. I feel like petting them before I do it. They'd like me to. Just look at them. Attention-starved. Not for children, though. They love me. They can feel that I'm on their side; that I'd do anything for them. A brown Alpine goat pushes its little damp rubbery nose against my hand and I kiss it. I inhale its night goat smell, now free of the scent of anxiety since the screaming kids are gone. I sense these animals don't particularly want to die. Not many people could do what I'm about to do. Most people have this delusion that they're compassionate. The popular sentiment is that life, no matter how lousy, confined or deprived, is preferable to peace. But true compassion takes courage and conviction, qualities that are often misunderstood.

It's quiet and insects are chirping and the children are away and I'm here. No wonder they're happy. But I can't stay here to keep them company and protect them; it's a nice idea, but not realistic.

I'm glad it's just me, and not Sunshine. Ravens specialize in carcasses but can be trained to kill animals and sometimes even do in nature, but this wouldn't be painless to the animals. She's had such a serene, death-free existence. This type of hands-on experience could be upsetting to her. It's one thing to drop a pretty silver-colored vial in a pet bowl. It's another to feel the excitement of animals being numbed, made happily tranquil and relaxed before they slip into torture-free and painless eternal slumber. Besides, I like doing it. The last thing they see is me; the last thing they feel is love.

~

I think Wanda admires me. I run into her at the ASPCA and tell her I have something for her. She says she'll stop by Saturday evening, before work.

~

I get a weird feeling this morning that things might not go so well when I'm hiding my girlie and detective magazines and one falls open to a page that says Shaquille O'Neal is doing Pepsi commercials. I mean, why Pepsi? Why not something healthy? Oh, who cares, anyway, advertisements only appeal to humans. Then it suddenly stuns me that a human could be so inspiring and beautiful. Wanda. She's too ethereal to be human. I think that's part of her appeal.

I'm giving my bangs a quick little trim—I put tape across my forehead so I cut a straight line—when Wanda rings the buzzer, thirteen minutes early. I guess she's anxious to see me. I buzz her in and then, since I have about a minute and a half before she gets to the door, clean out the sink with some tissue and then rinse it.

I open the door and Wanda's wearing pink, like an azalea pink, a man's shirt. It's a little big on her. I bet it would look good on me. I hope it didn't belong to that guy, that Lee guy, but why would a guy who wears a Megadeth T-shirt and kills himself wear pink? It seems like a healthy color. I think I'll get one just like it.

I invite her in and take her bag and put it on the kitchen counter, without even looking in it. Then I kiss her hand. Wanda blushes.

I pour us cranberry vodkas—why bother to ask what she wants, I made that mistake last time. Women like men to be assertive.

"Sit down," I say, "while I get something for you."

I could have had the picture right out on the counter, I'm organized that way. But I don't want her to think I hung out all day waiting for her. Besides, it will look more dramatic if I make an entrance. I'll pause at the doorway to the kitchen, take a deep breath—I've seen actors do this for effect—and then stride in holding the photo and place it in her delicate hands.

I watch Wanda's reaction to the photo. Her pupils are dilating, a sign that she thinks I'm handsome, or that she's excited. I can see through her like cellophane.

"Why, thank you," Wanda says, sort of stammering,

really overwhelmed by the gesture, I guess, and my Greek god looks.

"My father was Greek," I say.

Wanda doesn't seem impressed.

"This was taken at the Children's Zoo," says Wanda. "You're not holding an animal."

"You don't have to keep it in that cardboard frame," I say.

"I didn't think it was still open. After that incident," she says.

"I don't know if it is, why?"

Wanda takes a step backwards. "You were there, before?"

I guess this is a rhetorical question.

Wanda backs up, like she's trying to get away from me. Her soft flat shoe catches on the bear rug and she jerks her elbow out like she's trying to get her balance or catch on to something, and knocks over my lava lamp.

I rush to unplug it so we're not electrocuted and when I stand up the bear looks real, with its tongue flapping, about to lap up lava, glass and water.

"I'm sorry," she's saying. "Let me get that," and she pushes, shoves, really, the bear out of the way of the water and we see it trickling toward Sunshine's music hole.

Wanda gasps like somebody in a horror film. I feel angry and wound up. It might be the busted lamp, I'm hoping that it's the lamp that's upsetting me since the lamp was a soothing world, a peaceful place like sleep or the state you're in right before you fall asleep. But no, I'm not materialistic. I never thought I could get this upset over a person, a person I love, but it's happening now with Wanda. I love Wanda. I hate how I feel.

"You better go now," I say calmly, but Wanda's not looking at me. She's staring at the lava water going into Bruce's apartment, probably thinking I'm eccentric.

"Wanda," I repeat. "I think it's best if you go now." My hands are curled into fists so my nails, short as they are, cut into my hands and my stomach feels like a fist, too.

"Are you okay?" she says and she extends her long fingers, octopus tentacles of pseudosincerity. I can tell she doesn't like the photo.

"I'm fine, Wanda," I say, but I don't think I'm convincing.

Wanda says she's sorry about the lamp but I walk quietly to the kitchen to get her bag off the counter and this time, I look in it. I know it's rude to look through someone's bag but I can't help myself with that yellow glaring at me, like it's teasing me, and I reach in and pull out the clump of blonde hair. It's a wig. Underneath, I see black gleaming, the clunky black bug shoes and some little black leather thing, an outfit, a thong-type bodysuit with straps and chains, and then I see handcuffs and a whip.

"What are you doing?" Wanda springs at me, actually screaming, but this stuff she's lugging around like a foul secret is even more upsetting than her outburst.

"Whose stuff is this?" I demand, because it can't be Wanda's, Wanda who walks dogs every day and composes sad tortured music, uses Ivory soap, scents her drawers with violets and has a white clean apartment and takes off her shoes when she gets home, her toes are probably as long as her fingers and maybe when she's lying in her white cotton sheets she stretches her feet out and strokes her lemur and cats and rabbit with her toes.

I see gold glinting around Wanda's neck and then she starts to get shimmery, like a pink aura or a memory or a premonition, like I'm looking at her from far away and can't focus. I put the bag on the counter so Le Sang won't be tempted to swallow anything in it and Wanda gets still as I pull the words LouLou out from her modest shirt. I realize that LouLou is a stage name and that Wanda must be suffering terribly doing whatever it is she does in the wig and outfit at Les Gals. I look at her with genuine understanding and compassion.

The fan in the other room is humming. I can hear it clearly now that things have settled down.

"Please forgive me for flipping out," I say. "I don't know what got into me, please, here, sit down," and I pull out the chair.

I open my supply drawer to pick out a few things and compose a note to Wanda in my mind.

Dear Wanda,

I always knew I risked being misunderstood. My ideas are a little controversial. I'm aware of that. But I always thought you'd understand. I felt I knew you. I was wrong. Dead wrong. I thought you were perfect, Wanda. Well, nearly perfect, and now I have to deal with reality. When you love someone and you find they're sick and twisted and ruined inside, the kindest thing to do is to put them out of their misery.

Disappointed, but still loving, Pluto.